STEALING THUNDER

MARY CASANOVA

STEALING THUNDER

SCHOLASTIC INC.

New York Toronto London Auckland Sydney

Mexico City New Delhi Hong Kong

ISBN 0-439-17597-6

12 11 10 9 8 7 6 5 4 3 2 1   9/9 0 1 2 3 4/0

Printed in the U.S.A.   40

First Scholastic printing, December 1999

The text for this book is set in 12-point Stempel Garamond.

*To my writers' group, who helped me face the hard questions,
and for Katie, Eric, and Chas—for always being there.*

*Many thanks also to my editor, Julia Richardson;
my agent, Kendra Marcus;
and to the orchard workers in LaCrescent, Minnesota,
especially those at the real Apple Shed.*

CHAPTER ONE

Round and nearly full, the August moon shone on the Mississippi. It lit up sandstone bluffs riddled with rattlesnake holes. Bullfrogs croaked under its milky white beam. Like a search light, it flooded the highland apple orchards of southeastern Minnesota—as if showcasing the coming harvest—and crept into the Roselli's front porch.

Libby stirred on the porch couch. She pushed strands of hair from her eyes, reached to the wicker table, fumbled for her watch, and found it: 11:37. She'd slept—what—maybe half an hour? Suddenly wide awake, she felt the familiar feeling return. Free-falling. The way she'd felt since she found Jolene's letter in the mailbox, only four days ago. It was as if she were losing her footing, plummeting down a bottomless ravine.

She pulled on shorts beneath her cranberry T-shirt crammed her feet into her tennis shoes, and stood. Her breathing filled her ears. She listened for her parents, a footstep, a door opening. . . . Nothing. The house was quiet.

The words of Mr. Lenkin, her sixth-grade English teacher, rolled through her head: "Desperate needs require desperate deeds." She thought of her plan. A shiver tiptoed up her spine. She lifted the front door hook—glad that she'd chosen the porch over her hot upstairs bedroom—and silently slipped outside.

The air was bathwater-warm and sweetly scented with Jersey Macs, her favorite and always the first apples to ripen. Crickets rubbed their wings and pulsed high notes. The moon shone on the towering swallow house, which stood in the front yard, and painted everything silvery white: the three oaks, the gravel driveway and the orchard. Libby followed the edge of the crescent-shaped rose bed, walked beneath the oaks, then broke into a run. Dew on the grass soaked her ankles as she raced left and north between long rows of apple trees.

A brown rabbit zigzagged ahead of her, followed by a fox, its tail tipped white. She slowed her pace to watch them disappear—hoped the rabbit would escape—then ran on.

Breathless, Libby reached the white fence that divided her family's orchard from Northwind Stables. She placed her hands on the top board, its paint chipped and peeling. On the other side of the fence, her shadow waited, its shoulder-length hair wild as an osprey's nest. She could almost hear her friends Emily and Rachel say, "You brush Thunder's mane more than you brush your own." Well, they were at Girl Scout camp. For a while, she didn't have to worry about their opinions of her "mousy-brown" hair.

Libby stared at the glowing pasture. Her heart beat loudly in her ears. Maybe this wasn't a good idea. To cross the fence without Mr. Porter's permission, especially at night, would be trespassing, breaking the law. But in another way, it wouldn't. Not really. She was just going to visit Thunderbird, a friend. Jolene—for sure—would understand.

For three years Libby had cleaned out Northwind stalls, brushed down horses, polished tack—whatever was needed. In exchange, Jolene Porter had given her riding lessons, and in June, Jolene had occasionally allowed her to exercise Thunderbird—Jolene's favorite—the seven-year old Appaloosa who was too spirited for beginners. "You have a way with him," Jolene had said, as Libby rode around her in the outdoor ring. Jolene had smiled up from under her riding cap and red hair. "Or he has a way with you. It's never clear which comes first."

Libby thought of the neatly folded letter—a two-inch square—in her pocket. She knew it by heart:

Dear Libby,

We didn't sell Thunder at auction with the rest because Jim feels he can get more by selling the last three horses separately. I know how much you love Thunder, but we just can't take less than $5,000 for him. Thanks for all your help. I don't know when or if I'll be back. Sorry to leave without a real good-bye.

Hugs,
Jolene

With all the arguments about money she'd over-heard between the Porters recently, she knew they had to close the stable, but she hadn't expected Jolene to leave.

Since then, Libby had wanted to ask Mr. Porter's permission to see the horses, but his truck was always gone. She'd begged her parents, "Please, can't we buy him? We could fix up a spot for him in the old barn." On their other orchard, only three miles away, was a farmhouse and barn, still standing—barely. But her parents wouldn't budge. It wasn't only the money. It was harvest time, and the last thing they wanted to do, they said, was take on a horse.

As if a sharp stone were lodged in her chest, she ached to see Thunder. She climbed through the fence and glanced over her shoulder at the moon. Its cratered face mouthed "Oh," as if in alarm.

With two fingers to her mouth, she whistled. Twice. Then waited. The pasture glowed, and she could see clear across it to the training ring, paddock, and horse barn. Though the horses were usually brought inside for the night, she'd watched earlier, at dusk, from her bedroom window and saw them grazing. She hoped they'd still be out.

Pumpa-pum—pumpa-pum...

Hoofbeats drummed across the field. Libby turned. Galloping toward her, under waves of bluish light, raced Thunderbird. The Appaloosa tossed his head. His brown mane and long tail whipped. He ran in a wide arc, his neck curved like that of a warrior horse. Soon his dark socks slowed to a prance. His rump—a blanket of white with countless brown spots—marked him a descendent of the horses bred by the Nez Perce Indians. He stopped in front of Libby and whinnied loud and clear, his greeting rumbling deep in his chest. He pushed his muzzle toward her pocket.

Libby pulled out a sugar cube and let him take it from her palm. "One for now," she told him, "and one when we're done, okay?"

She touched his red halter, and shook her head. If Jolene were here, the horse wouldn't be put out to pasture with a halter, which could get caught on fencing. She patted his back; at fourteen and a half hands in height, he was neither too big nor too small. He trembled. "Whoa," she said. "Steady now." With both hands, she jumped hard, using all her ninety-two pounds of strength to muscle herself across his back, then swung her leg over.

"Walk," she said, without touching her heels to his sides. Gently, she grabbed a tuft of his mane in her left hand. He stepped into an easy gate. "Canter," she said. The Appaloosa gathered his legs, picked up speed, and shifted into a smooth rocking motion. The night was awash with smells of damp grass, the tang of horses, and ripe apples. She let go of his mane and held out her arms, as if she were flying.

At the clover patch on the pasture's western edge, Thunder eased up, settled into an easy trot. Then walked. "Whoa," Libby said. He stopped and lowered his head to clover.

She stretched her legs behind her, across Thunder's rump. She ran her hand along his neck; his hair was almost as soft as Mitts's newborn kittens. For the past two weeks—under the bench outside Thunder's stall— the kittens had curled beneath their calico mother, purring and mewing.

Time passed. Libby sat up on Thunder. Damp air clung to her legs. A breeze rustled the oak tops. Suddenly she shivered. "We better go back."

From the direction of the barn came a voice. "Thunnnnder!" It was Mr. Porter's, and he was using the surest way to lure in a reluctant horse—*rustle-rush-rush*—shaking oats back and forth in a bucket.

Libby groaned. "Oh, no . . ." Thunder pivoted, leaned into his shoulder, then bolted toward the sound. "Whoa!" When he was bridled, she could control him, but now Thunder lurched forward into a gallop. Libby clung to his back.

Libby glanced at the ground flying by and tightened her legs around Thunder's sides. The horse picked up speed, and flew across the pasture.

Seconds later, he came to an abrupt halt, nearly jolting Libby over his head, but she hung on.

Mr. Porter grabbed Thunder's halter with a jerk. Thunder threw back his head. His muscles tensed beneath Libby. She felt heat rise to her face, and wished she could vanish.

"Hey! Settle down!" commanded Mr. Porter. He looked up and yelled, "What kind of stupid. . . ." He pushed back his broad shoulders, and—in the controlled, molasses-smooth voice he used as a radio announcer on KQQR Country—asked, "Libby, just what's going on here?"

Her words got stuck somewhere between her brain and her tongue. "Um . . . I . . ." She tried to smile. "I'll put him in," she managed.

"Tried calling him earlier, but he just stared—

stupid as a cow." Porter shook his head. "Why we thought he'd be a prize horse, I'll never know."

Libby slid down and stood, finding her legs wobbly as a newborn foal's. She pushed her hands into her pockets and closed her right fingers around Jolene's letter. "He's just spirited," she said.

"He's got his own ideas, that's for sure." Mr. Porter gripped the halter beneath Thunder's chin, then yanked down hard. Thunder threw back his head—eyes wide, whites flashing. Porter yanked again, settling him. "But I got him now."

Leading Thunder, Porter stepped through the paddock gate toward the barn's back door. Suddenly, Thunder planted his forelegs, stopped abruptly, and pitted his strength in the loose dirt against Porter's.

"Hey!" Porter yelled. "You're not pulling that bull on me." He pivoted toward the horse, one hand still on the halter, and aimed a swift kick at Thunder's belly.

Libby opened her mouth as the toe of Porter's worn cowboy boot hit with a sickening thud. Thunder jumped sideways. Porter stormed toward the barn, and this time, Thunder followed him.

Like a quiet barn mouse, Libby slipped in behind them. She sank down on the bench between Thunder's stall and the tack room. Across from her, Cincinnati, the white Arabian, and Two-Step, the bay quarterhorse, hung their heads out of their stalls, watching. The other fifteen stalls were dark. Strangely empty.

Libby hung her head and squeezed her hands tight between her knobby knees.

Ka-klunk. Porter slid the bolt across Thunder's stall. "There," he said. "Now I can get some sleep." He tilted his chin toward Libby. "You get home now. And ask before coming over. Got it?"

"But . . ." Libby said.

"I know you used to help with the horses," Porter began, "but with only three, I can take care of them now."

Libby reached beneath the bench to Mitts' birthing bed, a wooden crate. She groped, searching for the kittens' soft fur, but she found only the folds of the ragged flannel blanket. She scooted off the bench, got down on her knees, and looked more closely. "Um, Mr. Porter," she asked. "Where are the kittens?"

Porter leaned against Thunder's stall door, arms crossed. "One cat's plenty," he said, scratching his unshaven face. "Too many and they spread disease." He paused to pull a cigarette from his white shirt pocket. "You ever see those animal shelters?" He snapped his lighter at the end of his cigarette, inhaled until the tobacco glowed red, then exhaled. "Sometimes," he said, smoke swirling with his words, "you gotta do what's best."

"What do you mean?" She rose slowly.

"You're not gonna understand, but just like on the farm over in Wisconsin when I was a kid . . ." He

—9—

jerked his thumb in the direction of the Mississippi, as if that explained everything.

Iciness flooded her. "Where are they?" she asked, her voice thin as skim milk.

"A gunnysack and stones." The cigarette glowed again, then Porter exhaled sharply.

She pictured the one white kitten, the way it had nestled under her neck, the way it had licked her palm with its pink tongue. Her mouth went dry. Her chest hurt, as if cinched too tight. She could have found homes for them, put ads in the paper, hung signs around town. She wanted to shout, to scream, to yell, but she turned away—throat burning—and took off through the barn.

She raced across the pasture, stumbled at a sudden dip in the terrain, and fell. She jumped up and ran on until she reached the fence, then scrambled through the boards. She stopped, and couldn't help but look back.

Beneath the yellow glow of the stable light, Mr. Porter shut the barn door, then walked toward his house.

Libby swallowed hard. The kittens. There was nothing she could do about them now. But what about Thunder? The whites of his eyes flashed in her mind.

In moonlight, she spun away and sprinted home through the orchard.

CHAPTER TWO

Libby's mom peered over the cereal box on the counter and sniffed twice. "You sure smell horsy. Thought you took a shower last night."

Libby sat on the oak stool, head down, munching.

"Horses must be in your blood," Mom added with a laugh. "The smell's comin' from your pores."

"Very funny," Libby said, hoping to throw Mom—who had the nose of a bloodhound—offtrack.

In jeans and a Roselli Orchards T-shirt, her mother leaned against the sink, grease marks on her tan wrists, black hair cut close to her head. "Libby," she began. "I wish we had the time and money for a horse, I really do."

"Not just any horse," Libby muttered. "Thunderbird."

"I know," Mom sighed, "buying a horse is just the start of the expenses. Besides, you don't have to own something to enjoy it, y'know. When we camp at state parks, we don't have to own the land to have fun, do we?"

Libby studied her cereal. Of course they'd had fun at Gooseberry Falls and Itasca State Parks, but that was different. Libby kept silent.

Her mother continued. "Even without owning Thunder, you have so much to be grateful for—all the wonderful times you've spent together. But we've been through all that, haven't we?"

"A thousand times," Libby muttered.

"Saying good-bye to someone you love," Mom said, "is never easy."

Libby wanted to tell her mother about the kittens and how the horses weren't being treated right. But then she'd have to explain being out last night.

The phone rang.

Libby's heart leaped. She glanced at the red wall phone and cringed. She hoped it wasn't Porter calling to complain.

On the first ring, Mom picked it up. "Hello?"

Libby curled her toes around the bottom rung of her stool and shoveled in a spoonful of cereal. How would she explain herself? That she'd been sleepwalking? Sleep-riding? She stared at the crossword puzzle on the back of the cereal box as if it were the most fascinating thing in the world. Her parents wouldn't be happy if they found out she'd snuck out after dark. It would shatter their "good girl" image of her. Just last week, when Libby's parents had friends over for a bonfire, Dad embarrassed her by snugging his arm around her shoulder. "Some parents constantly complain about their kids," he'd said, roasting a marshmallow. "With this girl, I'm always bragging. Libby doesn't give me any reason to worry. She's perfect." Libby had edged away from him. Sometimes her parents made her feel more like a puppet than a person.

"Uh-huh," Mom said, phone to her ear. "No, I'm sorry. We're not interested." Libby relaxed. Mom hung up and stepped to the sliding kitchen screen door. "Soon as you're done eating, come on out." The round kitchen clock showed 10:36. Libby had slept in. "Dad's been packing boxes since six-thirty. He has a few workers, but he can always use more help." Then she was gone.

Libby pushed away from the counter, rinsed her green bowl, and added it to the dishwasher. Heading upstairs, she ran her hand along the banister, her feet cushioned by soft carpet. She hurried past her parents' room, their clothes piled on their four-poster bed.

In the bathroom, white curtains fluttered at the window beside the embroidered plaque of the Ten Commandments. Guilt panged her. Trespassing. She'd broken a rule, somehow, but she didn't know which one. She scanned the small framed sign, relieved to not find a "Thou Shalt Not Trespass." She brushed her teeth, rinsed, and spit in the pedestal sink.

At the end of the hall, in her bedroom, Libby glanced out her dormer window. Apple trees stood like soldiers in neat rows, all the way to the white fence. The horses were not in sight. She had to see Thunder again, but she'd have to think of a way to sneak over in broad daylight. There was one way she knew of that might work.

She sighed, back-flopped on her bed, and smoothed her hands over the quilt's soft squares of pink, lavender, and light blue. The colors weren't her. Only last year, her mother had helped her redecorate. Grandma had made the quilt to match the lavender walls bordered by pastel clouds. Libby would have chosen brighter, bolder colors, but she hadn't wanted to hurt her mother's feelings.

On her dresser, fourteen plastic horses struck poses: rearing, grazing, running. There was a time when she'd play with them for hours, when they were almost as good as the real thing. Her chest tightened. She slapped the bed, palms down, and hopped up.

She returned to the open window. A warm breeze lilted through the screen. Legs splayed, a gray squirrel circled up the nearest oak. In the distance, the pasture was still empty. She missed seeing the herd: from Cookie, the twenty-eight-year-old pinto, to Sagebrush, the nineteen-year-old black mare with turned-in front feet. They were gentle horses—older, quieter—good for trail rides.

She couldn't let Thunderbird slip out of her life, too. She needed to be his owner. No. Even *owner* was the wrong word. It was different than that. More of a bond. Friendship. If ownership were based on love, not money, she'd be Thunder's rightful owner.

She changed out of yesterday's clothes, pulled on denim overall shorts over a white tank top, fastened the metal clasps, then stood in front of the antique vanity and studied herself in the mirror. Her face was changing. Less round and more heart-shaped. Honestly, she didn't know if she was pretty or ugly. Slivers of green sparked her brown eyes. Freckles spread like wildfire over the bridge of her nose. Her face was like meeting people at the Roselli family reunion last year in South Dakota; familiar yet different.

From one of the six small drawers, she grabbed a brush and worked it quickly through her hair. She pulled her hair back into a red barrette, let wisps fall where they willed, and hustled downstairs.

From the front porch, she snatched her tennis shoes, then sat on the outside top cement step. As she tied her laces, she looked for signs of her parents. To the south, seven cars were parked outside the apple packing building, where the fresh-picked apples bobbed in a giant "hot tub" of soapy water, then made their way along a conveyer belt to be waxed, polished, weighed, bagged, and boxed. Libby had helped plenty of times before. When she was too young to help, when she probably got in the way more than anything, she loved to shout "Echo-echo-echo!" in the adjoining room-size refrigerator.

In the distance, a car murmured north along the road, and turned at the Porters' driveway. She wondered if someone was going there to buy the remaining horses.

She jumped to her feet, hurried to the garage, yanked her black twelve-speed from alongside a tractor tire, and rolled it out. A monarch butterfly floated above the roses. Heat rose up from the gravel driveway. Libby glanced around, hands on her handlebars, and forced the pedals down—hard.

She'd be back before her parents noticed she was gone.

CHAPTER THREE

At Apple Blossom Drive, Libby veered left on her bike. Sun warmed her bare shoulders. A hawk perched on a white fence post, rose to the air, screeching, and flew off.

Libby scanned the Porters' green pasture for Thunderbird, but it was eerily empty. Last night's ride seemed like a dream. A good dream gone bad, that is.

Nearing the next driveway, she slowed, searching for any hint of Mr. Porter. Beyond the blue spruce, the stable doors—X'd white—were closed. To the right, at the end of a stone sidewalk, the Porters' chalet-style house sat quietly, flowers blooming red in the window boxes. In the driveway, a dark four-door was parked; the driver waited, elbow jutted out the window.

From behind Libby, to the south, the grumble of a vehicle grew. Louder, closer. Libby hugged the shoulder, waiting for it to pass. In a flash of glimmering teal, Mr. Porter cruised by, truck windows down, music cranked up. A stone caught air and hit her spokes. The truck braked, red lights glowing, and turned into the driveway, leaving dusty clouds. He *had* to have noticed her. She'd hoped he'd be at work. Then she remembered: it was Saturday.

Head down, shoulders shrunk forward, Libby biked past the two wooden poles that held the Northwind Stables sign, a carved wooden board with three galloping horses hand-painted in the top right corner. She passed by, bike tires humming, and fought down the tidal wave in her chest.

Beyond the three-foot hedge, a truck door slammed shut, and then it was quiet, except for the snapping, whirring sounds of cicadas and grasshoppers. The roadside was lined with purple asters, daisies, and black-eyed Susans. Ahead, the air shifted above the road, a mirage of water on the warm pavement. At the top of the rise, looking down the valley at the winding Mississippi below, she slowed. Just out of view of the stable, she stopped and straddled her bike.

To her right, the road gave way to a ravine, a thick, fern-carpeted forest where she rode on hot days with Jolene. Its paths were steep and root-woven, but shady and cool. To her left, the slope climbed toward the stable and orchard country, a region of rolling hills and deep valleys. A horse trail ran along the small creek, which paused to widen into a swimming pond. The pond was edged by willows, just north of the Porters' property. Many times, Libby rode alongside the pond and let the willows' long feathery branches brush her shoulder. Willows that were absolutely perfect—large and knotted, thick with leaves—perfect for climbing.

Perfect for spying on Mr. Porter.

She hopped off her bike, stashed it in the weeds, then hiked up the slope. The narrow path was branded with hoof prints. Only last week she and Jolene had ridden this way. She shook her head, trying to shake out her thoughts. She missed Jolene. There was so much she didn't know or understand. If she could only talk to her, get some answers. The first one: Why, really, did you leave? It all left her feeling empty as a hollow watering can.

Weeds tickled her legs as she ran along the path, sidestepping occasional mounds of dried horse manure. On the freshest mounds, flies lifted halfheartedly as she neared, then settled again, buzzing. At the next property, cows grazed on a far hill outside a stone-foundation barn.

A pheasant lifted from tall grasses, its long tail iridescent.

Free of algae and weeds, water flowed from the creek and pooled to a depth of five or six feet, then flowed on beneath the road and down the ravine toward the "mighty Mississippi." Libby hiked around its edges, scared a painted turtle from its log, and took cover in the shade of the willows. A mallard scooted across the water to the pond's furthest edge, flapping its wings, as if it threatening lift-off. But it didn't.

She glanced around—she was alone—then, nimble as a cat, climbed the largest willow, which arced over the water. Up past the rope swing, higher and higher. Libby found a notch that supported her back, then straddled the tree's arm and dangled her legs. The tree reached its roots into the bank and stretched above the white fence and stone wall, commanding a broad view of the stable.

The car was already gone. Though his teal truck was there, Porter wasn't in sight. Libby shrugged.

She hadn't climbed the tree since the Porters had moved in. When she was seven or eight she'd straddled the tree's largest branch, swung her legs, and yelled "Giddyap!" What a moron. Then she caught herself. No, she wasn't a moron. That was the word Emily and Rachel slapped on anyone they didn't like. She was just little then and loved horses. Dreamed of having her own horse someday.

She settled in and took up duty. The house and stable were about a football field's width away. Between the house and barn, the red horse trailer sparkled in the sun; the stable's name in brass letters arced along its side. When Mr. Porter first drove the trailer home, Jolene had danced around it. The cab was equipped with a bed, dining nook, fridge, and smelled of new upholstery. Jolene had invited Libby inside for a Coke.

And at the Mendota Horse Show, the new trailer brought as much praise as the horses. Whenever somebody asked about it, Porter would pat its glossy enamel as if it were the coat of a well-groomed horse.

Beneath the canopy of green leaves, a mosquito hovered by Libby's leg, then landed. She smacked it, leaving a bug imprint on her tan skin. Below her, sunlight dappled the ground like spots on Thunder's rump.

Part of her wished her friends were with her. And another part of her felt relieved—free—without them. Rachel and Emily were always part of the "in" group. Like magnets, they had the power to pull Libby in, seemingly as a friend, but—it struck Libby for the first time—they never really returned the friendship. Not really. At times Libby felt she was part of the group; but many times, she felt completely on the outside. Rachel and Emily loved to talk about music, boys, and clothes. If Libby mentioned horses, they rolled their eyes. "That's all you talk about," Rachel would say, shooting Emily a knowing look. Libby had learned mostly to keep her mouth shut. No wonder Thunder made such a good friend. He always listened.

Near the stable, a splash of movement caught her attention. Two-Step, the broad-backed bay quarterhorse, and Cincinnati, the smaller white Arabian, trotted from the pasture toward the stable. Mr. Porter was tossing hay over the fence into the paddock—not into the hay bins, which protect the animals from eating bugs and larvae with their food. The horses lowered their heads, eating. Then Porter walked to his house and stepped inside.

Libby wrinkled her brow and scanned the pasture. Thunderbird was still nowhere in sight. Something felt wrong. Her heart quickened.

Libby snugged her arms around her waist, waiting. Watching.

CHAPTER FOUR

Minutes later, near the pond's edge, something shuffled. Libby slowly drew up her legs. Branches fluttered below, followed by a strange sound—*thwuck-thwuck-thwack*. More shuffling, mumbling. Libby stared at the path beneath the tree. She held her breath. Leaves partially blocked her view.

"... Come on, baby, come a little closer, baby ... come a little closer to my love, ooooooo—oo—oo—yeahhhhhh ..." Singing painfully off-key, a boy about her age came into view. He carried a long stick, its bark peeled off, slicing at willow branches. Like a jungle traveler with a machete, he sent leaves and long grass flying. As he sang, he bounced his head; sun-bleached blond hair skimmed his ears. He stepped toward the pond and, just beneath her tree, gingerly poked his stick at the bottom. Seemingly satisfied, he dropped his stick and removed his faded blue T-shirt, then his leather boots, one worn toeless, then his socks. His singing turned to humming and he swayed to his own music.

Libby held her breath.

He started singing again. "Come on baby, come a little closer now, baby . . . oooooooo—yeaahhhhhh. . . ." Facing the river, he unzipped his jeans, slid them off his ankles, and stood in faded plaid boxers. With one last glance he hooked his thumbs inside the elastic waist and . . .

"Stop!" she yelled, as loudly as she dared.

The boy fell backward on his rear. "Hey!" Then just as quickly he sprang to his feet, grabbed his stick, and held it across his chest. "Who's there?" he demanded, his voice suddenly high-pitched. "Who's spying on me?"

Then she recognized him. Her mouth fell open. He was the boy who started at LaCrescent Elementary last April. Her grade. Rachel and Emily had thought he was really cute, but because during his first days there his ears turned red, her friends called him Dumbo. Now his blond hair hid his ears. Libby hadn't joined in the teasing, but she hadn't told her friends to stop either. One time, they'd teased about his living in a foster home until he slugged Rachel in the shoulder. Hard. A playground aid saw it and made him go to the principal's office. He got a week of detention. After that, the girls stopped teasing and instead just wrote notes about him. Rachel claimed him. "He likes me best," she said, running her hand through her silky black hair. "When he had to apologize, he looked me straight in the eyes. You can always tell." Libby wasn't so sure.

"Up here," Libby said finally. "It's just me."

The boy looked up with pale-blue eyes—eyes clear as a northern lake—then grabbed his jeans and began yanking them on. He was different in a way that made her insides swim. And somehow, a thousand times better-looking than she'd remembered. If her friends knew she was here with him, they'd die of jealousy.

"Hey," he said, squinting. "Stop staring. You could have said something sooner! I mean, do you get a thrill or something out of watching a boy undress? Are you some kind of pervert?"

Forget the eyes. "No," Libby said sourly, "you're the one who intruded on me." She pressed her back against the tree, locked her arms around her knees, and looked straight ahead. Maybe if she ignored him, he'd leave.

"You're just like my sister," he said, sitting on a log and pulling on his boots.

She stared ahead, but felt his presence. "Oh? How?"

"Crabby."

Libby didn't answer. Crabby? She'd heard sweet and nice before, but never crabby.

"She's not my real sister, actually," the boy continued, more to himself now. He laced up his boots. "Foster sister. She's always crabby, too—but Beth, my foster mom, she says it's . . ." The boy rolled his eyes. "Anyway, you're acting exactly like her. Hey, wait a second." He looked at Libby harder, studying her. "I *know* you."

Libby feared he'd connect her with Emily and Rachel. She jumped in, heading him off. "I go to—I mean, went to—LaCrescent Elementary," she blurted. "Junior high this fall, though."

"Yeah," the boy said. "I *knew* you looked familiar. You were always with those other two, kind of hanging your head. Followin' them like a puppy dog."

She swung her legs around and inched down the tree, her feet finding the branches and bumps she needed as a ladder. She dropped to the ground and faced the boy, who was dead even with her height.

"Listen," she said, arms crossed high, "you don't know me, so—so why do you want to put me down . . . call me a—"

He shook his head hard. "No, no. I didn't mean like a *dog*." He laughed. "I'm sorry, but you always hung your head, and your hair is so thick, I could barely see . . . anyway, pulled back like that, it—it looks good." He glanced at the tree, then reached quickly for his T-shirt and pulled it over his head, but not before Libby noticed his tan skin and shoulders. And at the fine soft hairs on the back of his neck.

"So—what are *you* doing here?" he asked.

His question startled her. "I ... uh ... my horse ..."
She struggled to sort out her thoughts. She let out her
breath and gazed beyond the rock wall, nearly hidden
by moss. "Well, it's not *my* horse actually." She paused.
"I don't think you'd understand."

Mourning doves cooed.

The boy didn't say anything. He picked up his
stick, slapped at the water, then began walking away.
Suddenly, Libby strongly wished he'd stay. Just a little
longer.

As if hearing her thoughts, he turned and reached
into his jeans pocket. "Uh, hey, you want one?" He
held out a pack of strawberry bubble gum.

"Uh, sure." A sliver of sun seemed to suddenly
burn the back of her neck. She reached out her palm,
then unwrapped the stick of striped gum and popped it
in her mouth. She looked back toward the stable. No
sign of Mr. Porter or Thunderbird.

"So what were you doing?" he asked. "Spying?"
He blew a quarter-size bubble of pink, then popped it,
drawing it back in his mouth.

His directness took her off-guard. "Maybe," she
said. "Maybe not."

"C'mon," the boy said. "You can tell me. I'm good
at keeping secrets."

A monarch butterfly lilted through the air between
them on yellow-and-black wings. Libby didn't answer.

With the flat of his hand, the boy swept his hair back, momentarily revealing a one-inch scar in the middle of his forehead. "Okay, then. Well, what's your name?"

"Libby Roselli," she said, suddenly shy. "And I already know your name."

"Yeah?" In his eyes, something flickered.

She remembered the day Mr. Lenkin put his bony hand on the new kid's shoulder and introduced him. All the girls sat frozen. "Griffin Kane," she said now.

"Just Griff," he said, and seemed to hold back a smile.

Suddenly, in Libby's mind, Thunderbird nickered, reminding her why she was there. She chewed at her inside lip. "Listen," she began. "I'm . . . um . . . really busy right now."

His smile vanished. A veil of coldness passed across his eyes.

She pushed ahead. "And I don't have much time. My parents want me to help with . . ."

A door banged.

Libby crouched down, hurried to the stone fence, and pressed herself against its mossy rocks. She watched. Griff scooted next to her. The sleeve of his T-shirt brushed her bare shoulder.

"I could have guessed," Griff whispered. "You're definitely spying!"

"I'm just . . ." Her voice faded.

On the back doorstep, Mr. Porter ran his hand through his hair, then stretched his arms wide, as if he'd just roused from a nap. He looked around. Libby feared he'd turn his gaze to the willows. But instead he drew his attention to the flower boxes beneath the front windows. He walked to the side of the house, returned with a green watering can, gave the geraniums a drink, and repeated this three times; then, seemingly satisfied, he walked up his steps and disappeared again inside.

"You're spying on a guy watering flowers?" Griff whispered. He turned away, hands behind his head, and leaned back against the stones. "You need to learn to live a little more."

"You wouldn't understand," Libby said, watching the house.

"Try me."

What would it hurt to fill him in? "Last night, he . . ."

"Who's 'he'?"

"Mr. Porter."

Remembering, Libby felt her chest fill with anger. "He kicked Thunder, my—well, I wish he was my horse. That was last night. And, well, it's daytime now. He did away with the kittens, and . . ." She realized she wasn't making much sense. "I don't know. I have this bad feeling. I owe it to Jolene to keep an eye on the horses—especially Thunder—even if her husband doesn't want me coming around anymore. But right now, I don't even know where Thunder is. He should be outside . . . with the others."

Griff scrunched his lips, then asked, "Didn't this place use to have a bunch of horses?"

Libby nodded. "Yeah, but they sold them off. The stable business didn't work, I guess. Just before they sold the other horses, the Porters were fighting—something about a bank taking everything away if things didn't change. That they could lose it all. Then Jolene—Mrs. Porter—left me a note. Said she was gone—maybe forever."

"Maybe he made her write the note," Griff said, eyes narrowing, "just like in a movie I saw once. He made her write it and then he killed her." He chewed at the edge of this thumb, then continued. "It's possible."

"Uh . . . I don't think so," Libby said, but his idea traveled down her spine like an ice cube. She shivered, pushed away the thought, and studied the house. Mr. Porter was still inside. If she risked crossing the pasture in broad daylight and got caught . . . she didn't want to think about it.

Her heart slammed in her chest, but she took a deep breath, and with all the calmness she could muster, faced Griff. "Wait here," she said firmly, then held his gaze. "Desperate needs require desperate deeds."

"What?"

"I mean, this will just take a second."

"*What* will take just a second?

Without answering, Libby climbed over the stone wall, eased through the boards of the white fence, and, determined to see Thunder, darted like a rabbit across the Porters' property toward the stable.

CHAPTER FIVE

Kicking up clods of dry manure, Libby raced toward the horses. Cincinnati and Two-Step swished their tails at black flies; they looked up from their hay mounds as she passed. Around the corner of the barn, out of view of the house, she paused to catch her breath. Slow her heart.

She glanced at the horses' water bin. Empty.

Libby crawled through the paddock fence, then hurried to the stable's back door. She squeezed the metal handle and stepped in.

For a moment, darkness blinded her, but gradually Libby's eyes adjusted to the dim light. Aromas of hay, manure, and horse sweat mixed together. She padded forward toward the shaft of light, which flowed into the walkway from the tack room's window. Eighteen stalls, ten on the right, eight on the left—all empty—except for one. The stall next to the tack room. Thunderbird's. His bulky form was in the shadows; he shifted uneasily.

"Thunder?" Libby whispered, stepping closer.

He nickered low and soft and shuffled in his straw.

She drew closer and raised her hand to touch the side of his face. But with a soft thudding of hooves over cedar chips, he backed himself into the darkness of his stall, blasting air from his nostrils. "Hey, boy," she said, her voice wavering. "What's up? It's me!"

She undid the bolt on his stall. In the gray light, she could make out something different about him. His right eye was tinged red. She stepped closer, and again Thunder nervously backed away. She had to try something else. She remembered Jolene's words. *Wait. Horses are the most curious animals in the world. Let him come to you.* She put out her hand, palm up, and instead of stepping toward him, she took a step back, away. "It's me, Thunder. C'mon, you big lug, you know me."

The Appaloosa shifted, took a step forward, and stopped. Libby waited. She studied his dark head, his eyes watching her. She held still. And it brought back the warm spring day when she first met him, kicking his back legs up as he raced around the pasture. She'd let him come to her then, too. Now Thunder walked up to her, nuzzled her hand, and licked her palm. Then he gently pushed his head into her chest, nearly squashing her against the stall's door.

"See?" she said, scratching him hard between the ears, just the way he liked it. "I'm not gonna hurt you." She talked softly to him and scratched him under his chin and along his neck. As he settled, she studied his eye. A small spot of blood tinged the edge of his right eye, as if he'd banged his head on something. It didn't seem to affect his vision. She'd have to tell Jo—

She caught herself. She'd have to handle it alone. Maybe there was something in the tack room for eye injuries.

She checked Thunder's water bucket inside his stall. Also empty. From outside the stall, she filled it from the spigot, then returned with it. Thunder dipped his head into the bucket, slurping thirstily. On the outside of Thunder's stall, hanging from a screw, was a crop—the stiff leather strap used to get a horse's attention. Libby hated them, especially the way she saw one white-haired woman overuse it at a horse show. One wrong move and the horse got whacked on the rump, over and over and over.

Libby hurried to the tack room, where Jolene's wooden desk was centered under a small paned window. On the right, English and Western saddles, bridles and bits lined the wall. The smell of leather, oiled and worn, filled the air. On the left were shelves of supplies: grooming buckets, each containing a curry-comb, a mane and tail comb, a hoof pick, and natural bristle brushes; Jolene had always encouraged her riders to groom the horses they rode, as she said, "to create stronger bonds." On the top shelf were medical supplies: ointments for cracked hooves, salves for fungus growths, and liniment oil for sore muscles. Many times, Libby had applied the small yellow container of Blu-Kote to small cuts and scrapes—to promote healing and prevent infection—but it wasn't for a horse's eyes.

From behind her, Libby heard something, someone, coming. Her breath froze. The sliding stable door creaked open.

Her legs threatened to melt. Hide. She had to hide. She moved the rolling chair, dropped to her hands and knees, and scuttled under the oak library desk. She pushed her back against the sharp desk legs, trying to squeeze herself into a tiny ball, arms wrapped tightly around her legs.

The barn light flipped on. Footsteps. Slow and steady.

"Horses! I swear, that's all she cared about." A stall bolt opened. *Ka-klunk.*

"Come outta there, you stupid animal!"

There was shuffling of hooves. She heard the snap of a lead clip, twice.

"Stand there."

Thunder's loud snorts filled Libby's ears.

"You and I," Porter continued ominously. "We're going to start seeing eye to eye, you got that?"

Whack! Crack! Whack!

The crop. Libby winced and closed her eyes tightly. Her heart slid from her chest.

Hooves thudded in the hard-packed dirt floor. *Crack! Whack!*

Stomach knotted, Libby couldn't bear it.

Crack!

She scrambled from beneath the desk onto shaky legs and stumbled out of the tack room, only yards away from Porter. "What are you doing?" she asked, voice wavering.

Porter froze, his arm raised at Thunder's head. With long lead ropes fastened to the rings on either side of the horse's halter, Thunder was firmly cross-tied in the walkway between the stalls.

Hot tears brimmed in Libby's eyes.

Porter lowered the crop, but held onto it at a right angle, like the end of a tennis racket, ready to smack. "This is *my* horse," he said firmly. "And you don't question how I handle my animals. You got that, young lady?"

Thunder's ears were pressed flat against his head. He strained away from Porter, the ropes taut.

"If Jolene were here," Libby began, her voice wavery, "she wouldn't let you treat—"

"Oh, well, if you know where she is, tell her to come home, will you please, and ask her to take care of her horses. You tell her that."

Libby found herself nodding. If she were Jolene, she'd have left, too. She stared at Porter.

"Y'know, I'm really tired of seeing you around.

Now get outta here," Porter began. He unclipped the lead ropes, turned Thunder into his stall, and added, in a voice suddenly calmer, "Don't make me press trespassing charges against you."

Libby couldn't move. Wanted to, but could not. She couldn't turn her gaze from Thunder. If she could just go to him, press her face against his neck.

"Can't you hear?"

Finally, her brain somehow connected with her body, and her legs worked. She pivoted in the dirt and bolted out the sliding door. Retracing her steps across the pasture to its north edge, she ran to where Griff waited.

She skimmed between the fence boards, scuttled over the stone wall, and slid down the mossy rocks to the ground. As she crouched down, tears rushed up unexpectedly.

CHAPTER SIX

Libby's chest shuddered.

"What's wrong?" Griff asked. He knelt beside her and lightly touched her shoulder. "Hey, did someone hurt you? Horse kick you? C'mon, you can tell me. What's going on over there, anyway?"

"It's just . . ." Libby rubbed her arms across her eyes, then wiped her dripping nose with the back of her hand. As suddenly her tears had started, they stopped. "He's hurting Thunder," she said. She drew a deep breath and exhaled. "I have to get home." She gathered herself, brushed the back of her bib shorts with her hand, and without another word, hurried past the edge of the pond and down the path toward the road.

"Hey, wait up!" Griff called.

Libby reached into the weeds for her bike's metal handlebars.

"Wait up. Did I say something wrong?" he called.

Then she pushed it to the road's shoulder, hopped

on, and pedaled. She left Griff standing there, calling after her. Her mind was jumbled, tangled as worms in a bait box. If she was much later in getting home, her parents would be filled with questions she couldn't answer.

Her bike flew down the easy slope, and she forced herself to look straight ahead, to not glance at Northwind Stables. Not even a sideways look. She didn't want to do anything to upset Porter more. He might treat Thunder even worse. Images of him hitting Thunder in the face with the crop ran through her mind. No wonder Thunder was acting strange.

A truck with wooden sideboards, labeled ROSELLI ORCHARDS, rumbled by Libby toward her driveway. Its driver, white-haired Mr. Wentzel, waved, hauling crates of freshly picked apples from their second orchard, a few miles to the northwest. The truck passed the Apple Shed, the red building where a handful of cars—locals and tourists—were parked outside. Most of the apples, however, were shipped off to grocery stores.

Outside the Apple Shed, Dad stood square as an ice block. His woven hat, the one he'd had since his missionary years in Guatemala with Mom, was tilted slightly forward. He was talking with the driver of a front-end loader. Both men waved as the truck pulled in and rounded the Apple Shed, heading to the packing plant.

Then her dad spotted her, smiling as broadly as his wave. "Hi, honey!"

Libby waved back, forced a smile. She veered away toward the house and garage, afraid he'd see her eyes and know she'd been crying. He was like that. He'd drop everything to make sure she was okay, to get a smile back on her face as quickly as possible. She put the bike away, grabbed an extra breath in the garage, then walked to meet her father.

He held a clipboard in the crook of one arm, and as she approached, opened the other arm toward her. "Mom said you disappeared." He studied her face, which she tried to shield with a lowered glance. "Everything okay?"

Telling Dad would make things worse. Like the time she'd fallen off the monkey bars in first grade and sprained her arm. Her parents led the fight for safer playground equipment. Now, every recess, nobody could play on the monkey bars unless a playground aid dragged out the thick blue mat. The "dummy mat," as kids called it. If she told him anything, he'd go have a talk with Porter. And Porter might not like that.

"I guess."

"Good." He paused. "Well, if you don't mind, why don't you give Ruby a hand? And don't forget, I'm keeping track of your hours. You never know, maybe you can save up to buy Thunder."

"But that would take me forever. He's for sale *now*, Dad. I saw a man over there earlier today. What if he was there looking to buy a horse?" She felt tears building and bit the inside of her lip. He didn't get it.

"At five thousand, he might still be for sale next summer."

She shook her head slowly. Though she wanted Thunder more than anything, it would be better for him to be sold to a good home—and as soon as possible.

"Keep a positive attitude," Dad said, patting her shoulder. "Things work out." Then, whistling, he headed back to the packing building, where he slipped through the clear curtain of plastic slats, which the forklift could drive through.

Positive attitude. Things work out. His words dug under her skin.

Libby stole a backward glance down two rows of apple trees to the pasture, hoping to see Thunder at the fence, waiting for her. But—of course—he wasn't there. Then she stepped under the Apple Shed's overhanging roof, between pots of yellow begonias.

Inside, rows of slanted wood shelves held bushel baskets, labeled from Paula Red, Beacon, Wealty, to McIntosh, Cortland, and Delicious.

A few customers milled about; the early season didn't keep them away. They sampled cut apples and dipped them in dishes of caramel sauce. They tasted Wildborough honey, which came from the valley, and apple butter. And along with sparkling apple cider, they bought apple-shaped cutting boards, apple stationery, apple bathroom scents, and apple muffin mixes.

Libby restocked shelves from the back storage room, helped customers weigh apples, fill baskets, whatever was needed.

Ruby Cather, who had to be in her seventies and lived in a tiny house in town, worked the cash register. She talked without stopping, bobbing her honey-colored hair like a chicken. "Real nice open house you had for your daughter," she said to one woman. "Oh, he's that way, Doris," she said to another, "but what do you expect? He's a McInness." She'd guess what kind of apples people would pick out. "Oh, I figured you were a Cortland man," she said to one young man, who didn't say a word in reply. Even with tourists, she managed to joke about the weather or a bit of current news, and she'd be laughing well after customers stepped out the door.

Libby's mom stopped in. "Hi, Ruby," she said, passing the counter and walking up to Libby. "I'm glad you made it," she said, hands on her hips.

Libby avoided her mother's eyes.

"Saw you come in on your bike. Didn't I ask you to . . ."

"I biked over to the willows," Libby said, choosing to be partially honest. She didn't have to tell her mom everything. "I was trying to check on Thunder." She looked up at her mother, wishing she could tell her how she'd snuck inside and saw Thunder cross-tied.

Tapping her lip with her forefinger, her mother said, "Fair enough. Next time, if you have plans other than what we've suggested, you better clue me in." She paused. "Or you'll be grounded. Understand?"

Libby nodded. "Okay." Then her mother left.

A few hours passed, and Libby's stomach grumbled. At the butcher block, halfway down the main aisle, she brought down her round apple slicer on another Paula Red, then set it on a plate for customers to sample.

As Libby popped an apple slice in her mouth, Ruby chimed, "Hello there! How's our favorite radio announcer today?"

Libby glanced up. A cold wave passed through her.

At the counter stood Mr. Porter.

CHAPTER SEVEN

White shirt sleeves rolled up, denim jeans hugging his lanky legs, Mr. Porter smiled broadly. "Couldn't be better. And you, Ruby, you're looking lovely today."

Ruby waved away his compliment. "Heavens." But her face tinted. "So, Jim, may I help you with something?"

"Lookin' for some good apples," he said. "Want to bake a pie. Whatd'ya recommend?"

Libby kept her head down and cut another apple, but from the corner of her eye she could see questions working through Ruby's head. Baking a pie—did that mean he was truly a bachelor now? For a rare moment, Ruby struggled for words. In the past few days, she'd wondered out loud about Jolene's sudden disappearance. "Pretty flighty, if you ask me," she'd said.

Finally, Ruby found her tongue. "Well, you'll want something a little tart," she said. "Right now, we just have two varieties to choose from . . . and I'd say you'll want Paula Reds . . . that's my bet."

"Whatever you say, Ruby. I'm putty in your hands. And spices, tell me what I need." He eyed the shelf of spices behind the counter. "I'm a greenhorn at this, but thought, heck, time to try something new."

Gag. Libby couldn't believe it. What a phony. He could sure turn on the charm when he wanted to. But Libby knew better.

Then he spotted her, and with a twitch of a smile, he walked along the creaky wooden floor to where she was standing. Libby inched backward, her thoughts racing. Wasn't there something she needed to get from the stockroom, a shelf that needed filling? But her legs were anchors.

"Hi, Libby," Mr. Porter said. His stiff cologne cut into the apple-scented air. He stepped closer, towering over her. He bent his head, his face only a foot from her own, and spoke rapidly in a whisper. "Hey, about last night—and this morning. Don't you worry. I'm not going to say a word to your parents about your being out so late at night and trespassing on private property."

"But . . ."

"I'm sure they wouldn't be happy. No need to upset them." He glanced behind him. Ruby was busy gathering apples and supplies. "And this morning—if you ever mention what you saw to Jolene, then I *will* have to talk with your parents."

Libby didn't say another word.

"Fair is fair," he whispered, smiling. "And from now, unless you're invited, stay away. Accidents happen." He held out his hand, his eyes drilling into hers. "Okay?"

Libby looked at his hand and almost against her will, found herself lifting her own. He grabbed her hand, squeezed it hard, crunching her knuckles, then closed the deal with one word: "Good."

"Got your things all ready," Ruby called cheerily from the counter.

"Okay," Mr. Porter said, turning and reaching for his wallet as he strode toward the counter. "What do I owe you, Ruby?"

Ka-klank-klang! The sound of a bike crashing to the ground came first, then the door swung open and Griff bolted in. He spotted Libby near the back and, eyes fixed on her, hurried straight by Ruby and Mr. Porter, then slid sideways across the polished wood floor toward her, nearly knocking her over. Libby tucked herself behind the butcher block. From his back pocket he whipped out a magazine, folded into quarters, and smacked it on the block. "We need to talk. I found this in his truck in town, parked outside the grocery store."

Libby shook her head at him and mouthed, "Not now!"

Griff scrunched up his eyebrows, not getting it, and plowed forward. "Anyway, I think there's something suspicious going on . . ."

She put her finger to her lips.

He continued, ". . . so if you'd let me in on what you think is happening over there at the . . ."

She inched closer, and with her heel, stepped on Griff's foot. Hard.

"Ouch! Hey, what's your problem?" said Griffin.

"What's going on back there?" Ruby called, using her retired schoolteacher voice. She'd taught high school English for a thousand years.

Griff spun around. Porter fixed a lukewarm smile on them. Ruby glared.

"Oh, nothin'," Griff said.

"We were just joking around," Libby added.

"Hey," Mr. Porter said, "better not be giving Libby any trouble, young fella. She's almost like a daughter to me. Right, Libby?"

Libby's throat went dry as sun-baked sand. The way he twisted things, his sarcasm, made her sick.

"Looks like I left her speechless." Then with a chuckle, Porter ducked through the door, bushel basket balanced on his shoulder.

Griff spotted the plate of sliced apples. "Hey, don't mind if I do," he said, dipping a slice in chocolate-caramel sauce. He popped it in his mouth.

Libby slammed the circular apple cutter through another red apple. White wedges fell away from the apple's core. She thought of how she'd shaken Porter's hand. It was almost as if she'd betrayed Thunder.

Disgusted with herself, she set down the apple cutter and wiped her hand across the front of her bib overalls.

Griff tossed his head back and forth, humming. He grabbed another slice, dipped it, and held it midair, en route to his mouth. "So, do you want to hear what I have to tell you?" He crammed the apple slice in his mouth and mumbled, "It-might-bree-'portant."

Libby glanced from Griff to the entry door window as the teal pickup backed away, then drove off. Maybe the apples were part of the way he twisted things. Had he really come for apples or just to warn her to stay away?

Ruby leaned against her counter and sighed. "He's so nice," she said. "Jolene should have her head examined, running off like that. Some other woman could just slip in while she's gone if she's not careful."

"Nice?" Libby muttered. "He's a jerk."

The back room door swung wide and Dad strolled in. "Who are you calling a jerk? Not me—or a customer—I hope."

"Well, he is," Libby said, chin high. She found herself trembling.

"Who?" Her father stepped up to the block, rested his hand lightly on the back of Libby's neck, under her ponytail. "Not this guy," he asked with a smile, thumbing at Griff.

Griff rubbed his forehead and looked away.

"Mr. Porter," Libby said.

At the counter, Ruby humphed.

"Oh, he's a good man," her dad said, grabbing an apple slice. "You're just sore because of Thunderbird. So—who's this?" Her father held out his hand. "I'm Libby's dad. And you're . . ."

With the back of his hand, Griff wiped caramel off his chin, and cleaned his hand on his jeans. Then he shook hands. "Griff," he said.

"I know what I'm talking about," Libby said sourly, anger threatening a meltdown. "He *is* a jerk. I hate him."

"Hey, now. *Hate*'s a pretty strong word, Libby. You shouldn't feel that way. You might dislike someone, but . . ."

"Oh, please . . ." Libby couldn't, wouldn't, stay around to hear the rest, about how we're called to love everybody, to see the best in everybody. She didn't care. Her hate for Porter glowed as hot as white coals. "I gotta get out of here!" she cried, and fled toward the entry door. She paused and glanced behind her. "Griff, c'mon." He followed. Left in his wake was her father, standing dumbstruck. Libby couldn't remember ever walking away from him before, having the last word. A pang of guilt swept through her.

She didn't turn back.

CHAPTER EIGHT

Libby aimed for the oak trees in front of her house and the wide circle of shade beneath, where a robin hopped, cocking its head at the ground. Griff followed a few steps behind her. As they neared the tree, the robin, its amber breast speckled with dark spots, flew off. Libby dropped cross-legged to the grass. She rested her elbows on her knees and propped her chin on folded hands. "So what were you trying to tell me?"

"This," Griff said. He opened the magazine, *Horse and Rider*, set it in between them, and stretched out on the grass.

"That's the magazine Jolene gets." Libby shrugged. "I've read it lots of times. Is *this* what you stole from his truck?"

"Borrowed," Griff corrected her. "I just borrowed it." He glanced up, hesitated, then met her eyes. "Listen, I don't steal."

"Oh," Libby said.

He flipped to the middle of the magazine.

Libby read the title aloud. "Horse Accidents: When You Have to Contact Your Insurance Company." With the article was an illustration of a horse lying on its side, a car and an alarmed driver in the background. The horse had just been hit. Libby's stomach knotted. "That's real cheery," she said, "but . . . um . . . what does this have to do with—"

"Does Mr. Porter read this magazine regularly?"

"No, I don't think so. They're always stacked next to Jolene's desk. Horses have always been her thing. He's more into drowning kittens, that kind of thing," she said sourly.

"I don't get it."

"Sorry. It's a joke. Black humor." Libby gazed up at billowy clouds. A puff of smoke curled from a dragon's snout. She watched the shape disappear, then turned to Griff again.

He leaned into his elbows and slid his palms back along his head, revealing his white forehead.

"Don't do that," Libby said.

"Why not?"

"I don't know. You look better with your hair down."

"Oh yeah?" His blue eyes lit up and a smile crinkled the edge of his mouth. "You think I'm handsome?"

He'd caught her. "No, I didn't say that."

With a smug grin, Griff turned his attention to the magazine. "Okay, I found it on the front seat, and your Mr. Porter was reading it—"

"He's not 'my' Mr. Porter."

"Whatever." Griff crossed his legs in the air behind him and tapped the worn edges of his leather boots together. "He must have been reading it pretty carefully, because the pages were creased open. Anyway, I figured I didn't have anything else to do, so I biked over to the library." The LaCrescent Public Library was only a mile from the orchard, downhill and just off of Main Street. "And I got on the Internet—jeez, I miss my computer at home—and looked up insurance and claims and horses and stuff, and that's what this is all about. A person pays insurance so that if an accident happens, they get paid something." He stared at Libby, as if trying to win a case in a courtroom. "But they have to prove there was an accident."

Libby leaned forward and whispered. "He used the crop on Thunder's face. I mean, a crop should never be used like that. That explains why Thunder's been so jumpy and why there's blood in one of his eyes. Does that kind of thing count as an accident?"

Griff shook his head, wrinkled his lower lip. "Uh, well, when it comes to collecting money, I think the horse has to be dead."

"Dead?"

"Yeah, a serious accident. Listen," Griff pressed,

"that guy, that Mr. Porter, there's something about him."

"Yeah, like all nice on the outside," Libby said, pulling a blade of grass from the ground and sticking the white stem in her mouth. "He does all these live-remotes on the radio for girls' basketball, which no one bothered to cover before, and he manages to do special interviews with celebrities. Ruby's in love with him, thinks he's a dream. Well, he gives me the creeps."

She picked up the magazine and read to herself: "No one wants to consider the possibility that their beloved horse could fall victim to a fatal accident; however, life deals unexpected blows." She read further. "To be prepared, always videotape your horse. Without photos, videotape, and records, it might be difficult to convince an insurance company of your horse's full market value . . ."

She stopped. "You know, Mr. Porter doesn't remember to even *water* the horses. He's not the type to read up on them. He just wants to get rid of the horses and . . ."

Griff's eyes met hers, and Libby sensed she could trust him.

She told him about how she'd gone riding in the moonlight and how Mr. Porter had kicked Thunder's belly. She looked to Griff. "So, if Mr. Porter was studying this article . . ." She could feel herself circling closer. "What I mean is, you're wondering if maybe he's thinking of . . . of faking some kind of accident . . . to collect insurance money?"

"Maybe," Griff said. "It's possible."

Libby paused, remembering a comment once from her mother: "They must be better at saving than we are," she'd said when Jolene had described their new hot tub.

"They're always buying new stuff," Libby said. "Did you see that horse trailer?"

"Thought it was a fire engine," Griff said with a wry smile. "How could I miss it?"

Suddenly, a steely awareness filled her. She scratched nervously at her ankle. If what Griff was hinting at was true, then they had to come up with a plan to prevent an "accident" from happening. And fast. But her head was empty.

She felt a warm trickle on her ankle and looked down. A small bead of blood formed on her skin where she'd scratched. With her thumb she wiped the blood onto the grass, then pressed against the spot to get it to stop. She thought of Thunder's blood-tinged eye and the way she'd seen Porter use the crop. A wave of dread washed over her. She had to protect Thunder. She had to find a way to keep him safe.

CHAPTER NINE

"I gotta go," Griff said, checking his watch. He then scrambled to his feet. "If I don't get the lawn mowed, then it's . . ." He made a slashing motion with his finger across his throat.

"Griff," Libby asked, stalling him. "Hey . . . um . . . why *are* you in a foster home, anyway?"

"Mmmm . . ." Griff shook his head, looked up into the oak, then said, "Guess I'd rather not say. Maybe later."

If he didn't want to say, that was fine. Maybe it wasn't any of her business. Still, she felt put off. Magazine in hand, she stood. "So . . . what do you think we should do?"

"I don't know. Call me. We can talk about it."

"But . . ." She wasn't in the habit of calling boys. "I don't know your—"

"It's under Wheeler—Jerod and Beth. But don't call past ten or it's—you know . . ." He motioned at his neck again. Then they headed to where his bike lay on the ground outside the Apple Shed. As Griff rode off, Libby trudged inside the house.

At supper, hoping to avoid conversation, Libby brought a book to the table (*Black Beauty,* by Anna Sewell, which she'd read twice already). She filled the tortilla with shredded chicken, lettuce, tomatoes, salsa, and sour cream, then folded it—bottom up, sides over—and held it in her hands. With every bite, she turned her head to read, but the tortilla slipped apart, its contents dropping to her blue plate.

"Maybe you should give up reading," her mom said, "at least for a few moments. Besides, I'd like to hear about your day. I was stuck fixing that old John Deere on the north orchard all day. Hardly saw you."

"There's not much to say," Libby said, keeping her eyes on the open page. Normally she'd sail through the story, but today she just couldn't concentrate. She kept thinking about Thunder. She stared out the sliding glass door, hoping to see the pasture, but rows of apple trees blocked her view. Was Thunder's life going to be the same as Black Beauty's, a series of abuse and bad owners? Owners that would never care for him the way she could?

"Libby?" Dad asked. "Libby. You okay?"

Libby glanced at her father, whose fork hung halfway between his fruit plate and his mouth.

Libby couldn't answer. Her throat was tight with

emotion. She picked up her book and pushed back her chair. "I'm not hungry," she managed. Then she headed upstairs—two steps at a time—flopped herself on her bed, and curled into a ball.

For a long time, she stared absently at the horses on her dresser. All she wanted was to return to a week ago, to the time before Jolene had left. When she could see Thunderbird anytime she wanted. It made her crazy. Angry.

She reached for her dresser and hiked up the volume of her clock radio. If she was going to start crying, she didn't want her parents to hear. The country station came on with a countdown of the week's top hits. They were on number twenty-seven. (Emily and Rachel hated country, but it had grown on Libby; it was the only station Jolene allowed at the stable.) It would be a few hours by the time they reached number one. Libby closed her eyes, but in her mind all she could see were red spots, like swirling molten lava, as she poured over the day's events. She had to tell her parents about Mr. Porter.

Between the eighteenth and seventeenth top songs, a familiar voice came over the radio to read a public service announcement. A country singer talked about the nationwide problem of domestic abuse. "No one should ever be abused," he said. "If you, or someone you love, has been the victim of abuse, please call the National Abuse Hotline. Someone will be there, waiting

to take your call." And then the message was followed
by Mr. Porter's voice, adding more information: "If
you're the victim of abuse," came his butterscotch-
smooth voice, "please call the national abuse hotline
or contact our regional shelter. That number is . . ."

The station returned to the countdown of hottest
hits. Libby stared at the radio. Had she heard right?
Mr. Porter had just been part of a public service
announcement about domestic abuse. Domestic abuse,
she knew, was about what happened in a home or family. Still, in her mind, animal abuse was pretty much
the same thing. Abuse was abuse, wasn't it?

Libby pulled back her comforter and without
changing, slipped under it. Who would believe her if
she accused Porter of abusing Thunder? No one.

Anger boiled up in her.

At him.

And at Jolene, for not staying and sticking up for
the horses. For abandoning them—and Libby.

She rolled to her side, closed her eyes, and let
waves of warm darkness sweep over her. Soon she was
drifting—riding with Jolene on a wide prairie. Wind
blew through golden grasses and through their hair.
"Let's race!" called Jolene, fiery-red hair and face
aglow. Their horses galloped, hooves soundless over
earth. Prairie gave way to dark and tangled woods.
They plummeted downhill and Libby yanked back on
the reins, but her horse wouldn't stop. Her horse flew,

jumping logs, bit clamped in its teeth, indifferent to her pulling on its reins. Finally, Libby's horse jolted to a stop at the edge of a ridge. Below was a dark swamp, thick with algae. In it, Thunder and Jolene struggled, trying to stay above water.

"Libby! Get help!" came Jolene's voice, desperate. Scared.

Libby looked around for a vine, a rope, anything to toss to them. When she returned her gaze, she saw Thunder's brown muzzle slip below the surface, then Jolene's hand. Algae swirled, covering the dark circle where they'd disappeared.

From deep within Libby, a wail rose up. "Nooooo!" She felt a vast darkness filling her. She sobbed, her chest aching.

Suddenly a hand was on her shoulder. Someone trying to console her. Libby pushed the hand away.

"Libby?" It was Mom's voice. "Libby, it's okay. You were dreaming."

Libby slowly opened her eyes. Tears flowed. Her chest still carried grief, a sense of deep loss. "Oh . . ." she said, sitting up and letting her mother hug her. "It was just so . . . so real."

"What was it about?"

Emotion cut off Libby's voice. She shook her head.

"With the good life you have," Mom said reassuringly, "there's no need for bad dreams, right? Your life is full of blessings. So much to be thankful for."

Libby felt herself bristle. She turned her head away.

"Anyway, it was just a dream," Mom said soothingly. She reached to Libby's dresser, then handed her a tissue. "Maybe you're getting sick." She put her palm to Libby's forehead. "You're not burning up. No fever. Still . . ."

Libby blew her nose, then took a deep breath.

A fever.

If only it were that simple.

CHAPTER TEN

Water swirled behind the River Queen paddleboat, a double-decker blue and white vessel, as it chugged away from its dock into the wider Mississippi. A sailboat, two fishing boats, and three speedboats dotted the sun-diamonded water. Seagulls lifted from sandbars, following. Libby wished she had something to toss to them.

She leaned against the stern rail, the noon sun pressing down on her bare shoulders. The floral sundress was her mother's idea. After the eleven o'clock church service, they'd driven through LaCrescent to the landing. The paddleboat cruise was a surprise. Her dad's idea.

"Something's been bothering you," Dad said, resting against the white rail and glancing at her sideways. "I can sense it."

Libby patted his arm the way he often touched hers. "I'm fine, really."

Downstream in the distance, cars glinted as they crossed the bridge between Minnesota and Wisconsin.

It was hard to believe that the river flowed on, on beyond the bridge, on and on, all the way to the Gulf of Mexico.

Libby scanned the shoreline, over pieces of wood . . . spare tires . . . things the river deposited on its banks. She took a deep breath of fish-scented air, relieved. Glad to not spot a burlap bag anywhere.

"Maybe it's boy trouble," her dad continued.

"Daaaad," Libby turned to meet his eyes. She laughed. "You mean Griff?"

"Well, sure," he said. "Seemed nice enough. A little jumpy, but otherwise . . ."

"Oh, don't worry about him, Dad. He's just a friend. I mean, we're not going out or anything." She smiled to herself, remembering last year when she'd told her parents that Ryan Reeves had asked her out and she'd said yes. They'd gone into a panic. "You mean dating?" her dad said. "You've gotta be kidding. Not till you're sixteen." Libby had to explain that "going out" meant that she and Ryan had told friends that they liked each other, who then spread the word. Their "going out" lasted eight days. She'd grown sick of Ryan following her around the playground like a puppy.

Puppy dog. Griff's comment.

"So it's still the horse, then," Dad said, arching his right eyebrow.

Libby pushed a loose strand of hair back toward

her ponytail. She looked up at sandstone bluffs, bluffs that rose to rolling green hills and valleys—and orchards. "Well, yeah. Sure. If you could slap down five thousand, I'd be pretty happy."

Libby felt a hand on her shoulder. "Time to be seated," Mom said. "They want to start serving."

"It's so nice out here," Dad pleaded, using his imitation little-boy voice, "I don't wanna go inside."

"C'mon," Mom said, tugging at his arm. "This was your idea, remember?" She caught Libby's eye. "What are we going to do with him?"

"Hmm," Libby said. "Throw him overboard?"

Her parents smiled and she followed them through the white-and-blue door to the boat's sunny dining room.

Seated at a window table with white linens, Libby worked on cracking the red shell of a crab leg. With a tiny fork, she pulled out the white meat, then dipped it in a silver dish of melted butter, which a candle beneath kept warm. "I feel like I'm tagging along," she said. "I mean, this *is* your anniversary."

Her mom shook her head. "We wanted you along. Besides, tonight I'm stealing your father away to spend the night at a bed and breakfast. That's my surprise to him."

Dad shot her a blank look, which soon changed to a smile. "Is that so?"

"It's hard to get him to leave the orchard," Mom

continued, her eyes still on her husband. "But I finally managed. Ruby agreed to stay overnight with you." She glanced at Libby.

"Sure, that's fine," said Libby. It made her feel secure somehow to know her parents were doing something romantic. Only last year, Emily's parents had divorced, and it wasn't easy on her. It suddenly struck Libby. Maybe that's why Emily was so big on teasing Griff. First about his red ears, but then she'd teased about his worn boots. And how he'd wear the same jeans day after day. Maybe she was taking her hurt out on someone else.

Her parents began talking about the orchard. Libby's thoughts drifted. What was Griff doing today? He'd asked her to call, but she hadn't. Three times, she'd picked up the phone, then chickened out. She gazed out the window. A red canoe with two paddlers hugged the shoreline, likely bracing themselves for the paddleboat's huge wake.

From the table behind her, a woman exclaimed, "I still can't believe it. I *got* the promotion. It's what I needed if I ever hope to get ahead. And God knows I need the money."

"Yeah, that stuff comes in handy," came the voice of another woman.

The first woman lowered her voice. "But you know who's going to be long-faced over this, don't you?"

"Ah . . . let me guess. God's gift to women?"

"You got it. Porter's really put on the shine the last month—working overtime, bringing in chocolates, being Mr. Upbeat. I thought for sure he'd get it—not me. Anyway, I'm sure glad Leiderstrom called people today. I mean, Sunday. Most employers would wait until Monday, but he said he wanted candidates to have a day to adjust to the news before returning to work tomorrow."

"That's pretty thoughtful."

"Yeah, a small-town touch. I'm glad for myself, but it sure would be tough to be passed over."

"A toast." Glass tinked against glass.

"To your promotion!"

"To my promotion."

Libby dipped another piece of crab, swirled it in hot butter, and popped it in her mouth. Then a chill hit her. In the stable. One of the Porters' last arguments was over money. When he learned that he didn't get the promotion, he'd be angry. Maybe desperate. And he might take it out on Thunder again.

Libby drew a deep breath. *He didn't get the promotion.* She shivered involuntarily.

"Honey, what's wrong?" Mom asked. "You look a bit pale." She leaned across the table and whispered. "Maybe it's—you know—getting close to that time of the month. Some girls get moody before . . ."

With a scolding look, Libby stopped her mother midsentence. In front of Dad? "Mom, please."

She sighed, unable to avoid her parents' eyes. They waited.

"Okay," she said, "it's this. I was just wondering, what would you do if you thought someone was"— her voice faltered—"hurting someone you loved?"

Dad leveled his gaze at Libby. "Tell someone, of course. Why? Are you . . . ?"

Libby shook her head. "No, it's not about me. I heard something on the radio last night. Made me wonder, that's all."

Her parents glanced at one another. The paddle-boat's motor hummed as the boat gently swayed.

"And is abuse the same thing—whether it's about people or animals?"

Her parents leveled their gaze on her.

"Porter drowned the kittens," Libby said.

Her mother sighed. "Oh . . . how sad."

"Sad," her father said, "but probably legal. You know I couldn't do that, but I suppose with barn cats sometimes people have to make hard decisions. Too many, and then there's the risk of rabies and . . ."

As her father talked on, Libby felt her meal turn in her stomach. Sweat broke out under her bangs and on the back of her neck. She suddenly pushed back her chair, hurried past the other diners and through the narrow door. She stepped to the boat's stern. Needed air. In the sun, she gulped a deep breath—once, twice—gazed down at the boat's swirling wake, then lost her dinner over the back rail.

CHAPTER ELEVEN

After hugging her parents through the car windows, Libby waved and watched them drive down the gravel driveway, then zip south on the road. She turned, stepped into the quiet house, and heard the phone. She kicked her tennis shoes off on the plastic doormat, then bounded to the kitchen, and picked up the phone. Griff, she thought, let it be Griff.

"Running late," came Ruby's voice. She was breathing hard. "Left my checkbook at home, and now I have to run back to the grocery store before I can get out there. But you'll be okay for a few minutes, won't you?"

What a question. Did Ruby think she was five? "Oh, sure," Libby said.

"My mind was somewhere else, down some other road, I guess. But I'll be there in a jiff, honey."

Libby said good-bye and hung up the phone. She wandered into the living room and turned slow circles in front of the coffee table. Even when it wasn't lit, the tall vanilla candle Libby had bought on Mother's Day smelled good. Closing her eyes, she turned slowly, something she loved doing when she was little. Not too fast as to fall down, just slowly, in place, with the house to herself. She tried to calm herself, collect her thoughts. But all she could think of was that she needed to talk to Griff. Had to call him.

At the thought, her heart picked up its pace, shifted from low gear to top speed. Her hands turned clammy. She stopped turning, opened her eyes, edged toward the couch, then flopped back into its oatmeal-colored fabric. A phone call, just a phone call, and it sent her into a panic. She needed to tell him what she'd overheard at dinner. They needed to formulate a plan. They? Why did she think she needed him?

"It's not that I need him," she said aloud, "but it would be easier . . ." She hadn't needed Griff that night when she'd taken Thunder for a ride alone—she was brave enough for that—but that was before she'd angered Porter. Calling Griff, actually picking up the phone and calling him felt so . . . so direct. Bold. Her heart raced again. No matter. It was Thunder she needed to be most concerned about, not her stupid fears. She swallowed, rubbed her damp palms together, then pushed herself off the couch and forced her legs toward the kitchen.

Her hands trembled as she thumbed through the

slim phone book, found the number, and without pausing to lose her courage, dialed. On the first ring, Griff answered. "Hello? Uh, I mean, Wheelers', Griff speaking."

Libby pressed her back against the wall, phone to her ear. "Griff?" she asked, catching herself. Of course it was him. He'd said so.

"Yeah? Libby?"

Her heart raced, but she tried to keep her voice steady. "Uh-huh. Anyway, here's the thing," she said, "I wouldn't have called you, but—"

"Why *wouldn't* you call me? Am I that bad?"

"Noooo . . . it's just . . . just . . ."

"Yeah?"

"Just listen, okay?"

"Okay. You have my undivided attention."

She told him what she'd learned about Porter at dinner. About her fears of what might happen.

"If he didn't get that promotion," Griff said over the phone, voice muffled, "then the fireworks could begin. If he drinks heavy, then no doubt about it."

Libby tried to remember if she'd ever seen Porter drink. "I've seen him with a beer a few times, like after a horse show, but nothing too serious." Libby's stomach tensed. Porter didn't need to be drunk to be mean-spirited.

Over the phone, they formulated a simple plan: first, Griff would join Ruby and her for a bonfire, then return later to go over to the stable. They wouldn't actually steal Thunder, but they'd get him to a place of safety.

"Hello? Anybody home?" Ruby called from the front door.

"Gotta go," Libby whispered, hung up the phone, and felt heat rise to her cheeks.

"Look like you swallowed a canary," Ruby said. She picked up the green teakettle, filled it at the faucet, returned it to the stove, then cranked the gas burner beneath it. From her shoulder bag, Ruby pulled out a lemon mist tea bag. She never went anywhere without them. "Stood there at the checkout, all my bags loaded up, and couldn't find my checkbook. Gosh, it was embarrassing."

Libby sat across from Ruby at the counter and pretended to listen; inwardly, part of her smiled. She reviewed her conversation with Griff. They had a plan.

The bonfire, built in the stone fire pit a few yards from the back deck, blazed up toward emerging stars. In the flames, birch logs sizzled. Smoke curled and danced, weaving and snaking, up to the canopy of midnight blue. The moon, low and glowing like a round white platter, inched higher on the horizon.

Libby sat between Ruby and Griff, each on their own log around the fire, roasting marshmallows for s'mores.

"Life is so easy when you're a kid, huh?" Ruby said, her pink sweatshirt reading SIXTY SOMETHING.

"Oh, yeah," Libby said, shooting Griff a glance. "It's a breeze."

"So," Ruby said to Griff, "I hear you're living with Beth and Jerod. How's that working out?"

Knowing Ruby, she'd probably spent the last day making phone calls, finding out Griff's entire life history. Libby turned her marshmallow slowly above red coals until it was golden. Without warning, it burst into flames. She blew on it frantically, putting out the tongues of fire, but then the black charred marshmallow drooped from the stick and fell to the ground. She groaned.

"Oh, they're strict," Griff said, sliding his golden marshmallow off a sharpened stick between two graham cracker halves. "Perfect," he said to Libby. Chocolate melted at its edges. Then he continued talking to Ruby. "You'd think I was asking for a Hummer or a Corvette when I asked to stay here until ten-thirty. It's usually a nine o'clock curfew."

"They called me to double-check," Ruby said. "They're good folks. Take in lots of foster kids. I used to get to know a few through school. Some would say troubled kids, but I figure it's usually good kids in some troubled situations. That's how I always tried to see it."

Libby played in the fire with her stick, watching

the bits of leftover marshmallow blacken to ash.

"Yeah," Griff said quietly, head down. "Some people are good, and some aren't worth knowing."

"Oh, like who?" challenged Ruby. "I can learn to like just about anybody, no matter how much I start off hating them. Just got to get to know a person, that's all."

"You never met my parents," Griff said. He stared at the fire and half-covered his mouth with his hand, as if to hold in his words. "They say it's good for me to talk about it." Hand in place, he explained how he went to counseling and that his parents were both in treatment at Hazelden for alcoholism. Until things got better, the state had placed him in foster care. "I came with a file and a list of warnings." He laughed to himself.

"Warnings?" Libby asked. She waited with sudden dread.

He shrugged and tilted his head. "Oh, stuff. Like—I have to see a counselor every month—they must think I'm going to flip out again, but who wouldn't, if you woke up and found both parents passed out cold . . ." He stopped talking, and stared into the fire, then spoke again. "I mean, it's not like it happened only once . . ."

Libby couldn't imagine it. She hoped things worked out for Griff. It had to be tough. She didn't know what to say.

"Life deals a lot of screwball cards sometimes," Ruby said. "It's our job to do the best we can with the cards we've been dealt."

Libby thought of Jolene. "Or protest," she said, "and demand a redeal."

Ruby laughed, but Griff was lost somewhere in thought, staring at the embers. The fire died to dull coals as the moon climbed steadily higher.

Finally, Ruby shifted on her log, yawning. "Better get some sleep. Gotta open up tomorrow morning. Time to call it quits, kids."

Libby stretched. "Yeah, I'm pretty tired."

Ruby looked at her sideways. "Tired? I thought kids your age were never tired."

Libby gave a laugh, but inwardly grimaced. If she weren't more careful, Ruby'd suspect something. She pretended to yawn.

Scritch. Scritch. Scratch.

Libby bolted upright in her sleeping bag, fully dressed in a navy sweatshirt and shorts. The noise—a scratching—where was it coming from? She remembered a mouse once, caught in a trap, half-alive, dragging the trap around the kitchen. Skittering, scratching. She struggled to open her eyes.

"Libby, wake up," came Griff's voice.

She pushed her hair off her face and tried to focus.

Pressed against the front porch screen was a flattened face, nose, and lips. It was Griff. "C'mon."

"Okay," Libby whispered. "I'm awake—I'm awake." In an instant, she grabbed the yellow flashlight she'd shoved under the sofa, tied on her tennis shoes, and was out the door, tiptoeing down the cement front steps. She pressed the glow button on her watch: 3:35.

Pale moonlight—for the second night in a row—lit up the orchard as if it were a stage, lights up, curtains drawn. Without a word, Libby led the way between squat apple trees toward the white pasture fence. They crouched, the dew thick on the grass.

Hoooo-hooooo-hoo-hoo!

"What was that?" Griff said, his voice shooting higher.

"Just an owl." She hoped this owl wasn't some sort of bad omen. A good omen. That's what they needed.

In the distance, to the right of the stable, a soft light lit the kitchen of the Porters' house. Though the barn light was off, a path of white moonlight illuminated the field. They had to make their way to the stable without being seen. In and out, that was the plan. Straightforward. Simple.

Libby's palms were sweaty and cold. She swallowed hard.

She scanned the Porters' property. She missed seeing Jolene's car. The truck was parked and the house was dark. It was the sign she needed to scramble through the fence boards.

"Okay," she whispered, "follow me." Emboldened, she raced across the pasture; her legs wobbled as they hit uneven ground, then propelled her forward again. Griff was at her side, his hair like a white helmet in the pale light.

Libby slowed and rounded the barn. She clicked on her flashlight and tried the pasture door. It wouldn't budge.

They'd have to go around front, toward the driveway and house. She motioned with her arm for Griff to follow. As she made her way past the water trough, avoiding fresh horse piles, a light breeze whipped up, rushing through the treetops surrounding the house. *Shoooosh—shoooosh.* Griff's breath was right behind her.

Somewhere far off, a dog barked.

Libby eased around to the stable's front door, slid it open by a foot—it creaked—and she slipped in, closing the door behind them. Mitts brushed alongside her leg, looking up at her with glowing amber eyes.

"Hi, Mitts," she whispered. "Haven't seen you in a few days."

Except for a moonbeam cutting through the single window, the darkness in the stable was complete. The rich scent of hay and manure permeated the air.

"Thunderbird?" she whispered.

A rustle of straw, a snort, and then a nicker. She moved toward his stall. With a rumble, Thunderbird rose from his bed of straw and shook his coat. Libby inched closer and found him stretching his neck over his stall door. She pressed her face to his cheek, then flashed her light along his sides, his legs. His eye was still red. "We're gettin' you outta here."

She went to the tackroom and found his bridle on the right wall. For now, that would have to do. She'd have to find a way to get oats, a salt lick, grooming supplies, and other things—later.

Quickly, she eased into his stall. Thunder shifted, backed up again uneasily. Libby waited calmly for him to step to her.

"Hurry," said Griff. He tapped his fingers on the stall door.

"Hang on," Libby whispered. Finally, Thunder inched closer, took the sugar cube she held in her palm, and let her stroke his neck, then slip a bridle on him. She led him down the walkway and out the barn's back door to the pasture. Cincinnati and Two-Step watched from their stalls and nickered as they headed outside. She hated to separate them—horses were herd animals—but what else could she do?

In the paddock, Thunder shook his coat.

Libby had no idea how long she could keep Thunder safe. As long as necessary. That's all she knew.

CHAPTER TWELVE

Clouds crossed the moon's face. While Griff ran back for his bike at her house, Libby rode Thunder to the west end of the pasture. She unlatched the corner gate, held it wide with her foot, and rode out. Then she cut back along the north edge of Porter's property, edged the pond and willows, and found the dirt path. Far off, a car rumbled; its lights swept over the hill, and it sped swiftly past, leaving cricket song in its wake.

Griff stood up from the weeds—a shadowy form— and combed his hand through his hair. "I'm right here," he said. "Don't trample me." Then he rolled his bike from the weeds to the road's shoulder.

Thunder snorted, flapping air hard through his nostrils, and shifted his feet uneasily.

"It's okay," Libby said, and patted the horse's neck. "It's just Griff." Just Griff, she thought, as though they were old friends. Strangely, though she'd only known him a short time, she felt more at ease with him than with Emily and Rachel. It was if he accepted her just the way she was. He wasn't waiting for her to measure up somehow. She glanced over her shoulder at the empty road, thankful no car lights were headed their way. "Ready?" she asked.

"Always." Griff pushed his bike onto the road's shoulder, hopped on, and began pedaling north along the road. Libby rode in the ditch, keeping pace alongside. She trusted Thunder to find his footing. The road curved, dipped, and climbed. They passed fields, the Bancroft feed store, and several driveways leading to newly constructed homes.

Stone-faced, cows ambled silently to a fence and watched.

"Don't tell anyone you saw us," Libby told them, and for the first time, she felt good. Good to know she was saving Thunder. Good to know that she'd stood up for what was right. But like water on hot pavement, the feeling quickly evaporated. Was she going against everything she'd been taught? *Thou shalt not steal.*

Libby glanced behind, expecting to see Porter's truck or the police. "Griff," she said, "once Thunder's safe, we should go to the police. Tell them how Porter treats him, and you could back me up. You know, two against one. Maybe they'd let me care for Thunder, kind of like foster care, until Porter shapes up."

"That's a good one," Griff said, and blew a whistle of air. "They'd never believe *me.*"

"Why not?"

"I stole a car once, that's why."

As if she'd cracked her head on a steel beam, Libby drew Thunder to an abrupt stop. She turned to look at Griff, who slowed down and straddled his bike. "You what?" she said.

"I was eleven," Griff explained. "Angry at my skunk-drunk parents, so I took their keys and drove their station wagon into the lake."

Libby didn't know if she should be shocked, or laugh.

"Straight in. Deep. Parked it there. I know it was stupid. I had to go to juvenile court, the whole nine yards."

She didn't know what to say. What in the world was she doing out here in the middle of the night on this rescue mission—with this kid? A criminal? So much for the idea of turning to the police. They'd have to do this alone.

"Griff," she asked, "if we get caught, would they send us to prison?"

"No . . . not an adult prison, anyway. A juvenile facility, maybe."

"Thanks. Makes me feel a lot better," she said, only slightly sarcastic. "When you drove that car in the lake, did the police come and take you away? I mean, what happened?"

Griff pushed down on his pedal and began again.

Libby lifted Thunder's reins and he resumed his steady pace through the ditch.

"Oh," Griff said, "I was supposed to meet with my parents at the law enforcement center, but when the time came, they weren't sober enough to show. So I just walked over by myself. One guy, I can't remember his name now, he was actually pretty decent. I mean, he listened to me. Something my parents never did."

"My parents don't listen either," Libby said. "I mean, they say I'm great and they don't worry about me and all that, but they don't really listen to me, or take me seriously. I tried to explain that if I didn't buy Thunder soon, he'd be sold. That I want him more than anything. My dad just says, 'oh, he might still be available next summer.'" She huffed. "They don't get it. I wanted to tell them about the way Porter was treating Thunder, but . . . I didn't bother. They'd think I was exaggerating so I could get him. They hear what they want to hear."

"Yeah," Griff said. "I know how it goes."

In the distance, floodlights lit up the Smithen Orchard. As they neared the light, Thunder began to weave, sidestepping.

"Hey, fella," Libby said. "It's okay."

Ahead, in the light, something silver shimmered in the grass. The breeze lifted it a foot in the air, then dropped it.

Thunder threw his head—spooked—and jumped

sideways. In the same moment, Libby flew off Thunder's back, and through dark nothingness. Her left foot hit the ground with a crunch, then arms spread, she landed facedown, flattened like a pancake. Her breath slammed from her lungs. "Oooof!"

"Hey, you okay?" Griff asked. "You flew like a monkey . . ."

Libby struggled for air, but it felt like one of the horses was standing on her chest. Finally, she wheezed in a giant gulp. A warm breath touched the back of her neck. Her arms found Thunder's familiar soft muzzle, then his warm neck. A numbing sharp pain surged through her foot, but she rose to her knees, and looked around. They were right under the floodlight's wide beam. At the farmhouse across the road, the house lights were out. She rose to her right foot, steadied herself, and grabbed Thunder's reins. He snorted again and eyed the fast-food wrapper on the ground.

"Libby?"

"I'm fine," she managed, jaw clenched. Hot pain flooded her foot, but she hopped toward the next culvert, a metal round tube, and made Thunder stand below. "Stand," she said, slipping his reins over his neck. Partly hopping, partly crawling, she hobbled up the short incline to the top of the culvert and stood nearly level with his back. "Easy," she said. "Don't take off, please." She placed her hands on his withers, and with a wince, slowly swung her left leg and foot

over his right side—the only way she could manage—
and was back on.

"Let's bolt," Griff urged, pressing down on his
pedal. "Somebody might spot us."

Libby pressed her knees lightly into Thunder's
sides. He swooshed rhythmically away from the light
and through long grasses. *Swoosh-a-woosh-woosh.*
They rode on through moist air. Within minutes, the
pain in Libby's foot grew unbearable, and she
squeezed her eyes shut. When she opened them, a sliver of sunlight pierced the charcoal shadows. The sun
was already rising. They had to keep moving. From
the weeds, a brown rabbit darted out and crossed the
road. This time Thunder didn't flinch.

Farther ahead, they passed a tiny house with toys
scattered across its fenced front yard. Suddenly, from
the house, barking erupted like artillery.

"Hope they keep that mutt inside," Griff said,
glancing over his shoulder.

Libby gripped her thighs harder around Thunder's
back. She followed Griff's gaze.

A houselight flicked on and the front door opened.
From the top step flew a German shepherd. A robed
woman stepped out. "Oh, no! Get back here, Charger!
Charger!" In a flash, the large dog shouldered through
the open metal gate, feet churning gravel.

A shot of fear pierced Libby's gut.

Thunder side-stepped, then bolted ahead, nearly

flinging Libby backward, but she managed to regain her balance, lean forward, and hang on. Griff slammed on his pedals, swore, and propelled the bike faster down the road's curving slope.

The dog's bark was deep. It sounded as if it could swallow three pounds of horseflesh in one bite. He grew louder. Right behind Thunder. Libby inched her knees higher along Thunder's sides and stole a quick backward look. Snapping, the dog's teeth glinted only inches behind. Thunder lurched, and the dog yelped. Abruptly it dropped back. Its yelps turned to faint echoes.

After they reached the bottom of the hill and neared the top of the next, Libby moved her hand forward on the reins and gradually eased in, slowing Thunder to a canter. "Trot," she said, her throat dusty dry, and he obeyed. She patted his sweaty neck, then wiped her hand on her jeans. "Oh . . . that was close."

"Yeah, too close." Halfway up the next rise, Griff paused, face red. "What do you think made the dog stop?"

"Thunder kicked him."

Her foot throbbed. Almost there, she told herself.

At the crest, sun spilled over the horizon. It cast a pale light on the valley, a green rumpled blanket sloping toward the river.

With each plodding movement, the pain grew. As did the guilt. What was she doing? Thunder wasn't hers. She *was* stealing. And Griff. A juvenile record. She swallowed hard. As if she had many good options. She pushed the nagging thoughts into the corner of her mind, gritted her teeth, and cantered Thunder the last half mile.

"Hey!" Griff called from behind.

At an unmarked gravel road, she waited for Griff to catch up, then they followed the narrower road along sandstone outcroppings to a wide stream. "Whoa," Libby said, and let Thunder step from the road to drink. He slurped noisily.

"Y'know, we're fugitives," Griff said.

"What'dya mean?" Libby glanced down from Thunder's back.

"Criminals. Running from the law."

"We are not," Libby stated. "We're protecting Thunder." When Thunder was done drinking, she turned him back onto the road and continued on. Griff followed. "Robin Hood and Fair Maid-what's-her-name—rescuing a lowly horse," he said, biking along-side.

Libby would have laughed, but she couldn't.

Around the last bend, the road widened into a dead end beside a small wooden sign, lettered white: ROSELLI ORCHARDS. Beyond, grasses nearly swallowed a small farmhouse, which had lost its windows and doors. A sapling grew through its front porch boards. Behind it, a large wood-sided barn leaned wearily; on its crest sat a large tin cupola like a tarnished crown. Surrounding the barn, as far as the eye could see, grew row upon row of apple trees. Tire ruts marked the grasses. Beside a newer shed, empty wooden crates were stacked three deep.

"We have to hide him fast," Libby said, "before the pickers show up." Early morning was the best time to start picking, before the heat turned sweltering. Many times, Libby had worn a red cloth basket with shoulder straps and had filled it to brimming. She knew how to give each apple a quarter twist and then lift up so it dropped freely into her hand. She knew of blisters and branch scrapes and sore shoulders. If she was forced to flee with Thunder, she could always make money picking at orchards.

Griff took in the layout of the orchard. "Isn't the barn kinda obvious?"

Libby slid off Thunder onto her good foot. Pain seared through her left one. She gripped Thunder's reins, and hopping, made her way to the barn.

"Bet this place hasn't been used for years," Griff said.

Like loose ribs on a whale skeleton, a few side boards had fallen away from the building. Libby bit down on the soft inside of her lip. Until they came up with a better hiding spot, it would have to do.

CHAPTER THIRTEEN

Like cannon shots, cracks of thunder sounded. Beyond the western edge of the upper orchard, black clouds formed a massive wall. Wind combed through the grasses, hiding their recent path made by hooves and bike tires.

Outside the barn Thunder flattened his ears, but Libby held him firmly. As she did, Griff worked a stick under the door's rusty lock until the whole thing pulled away from the weathered wood and thudded to the ground. Then he heaved the door open over grassy earth, let Libby and Thunder pass through, and pulled it shut behind them.

Gradually, Libby's eyes adjusted to the near darkness. The barn smelled stale. Libby's nose itched from the layers of dust. *Plink-tink-tink.* Rain danced on the roof. One-legged, Libby hopped ahead, leading Thunder.

Cobwebs feathered corners. A cement platform ran

through the barn's center with steel pipes—a cow stanchion—and old horse harnesses hung on one wall. In the back of the barn, beside two stalls, she dropped the reins. "Stand," she said.

One stall held the remains of an old tractor. Libby hopped into the other stall, pulled out a broken spindle chair from the earth floor, then turned Thunder in. "You'll be okay here," she said, patting his neck. She found a hook outside the stall gate.

Lightning crackled overhead and glowed outside the small barn windows. Thunder shook his mane, trotted a tight circle in his new stall, then pawed repeatedly at the floor. The storm rattled the barn, and wind whistled through the side boards.

"This barn gonna hold together?" Griff asked, one hand on a barn post opposite the stalls. Rain pounded down. "So how are you going to feed him?" Griff asked, then let out a long yawn. "We'll, what, come back later with oats and stuff?"

Libby shook her head, then nodded. She was having a hard time concentrating. She dropped into the chair beside Thunder's new stall. "I've gotta sit," she whined. "My foot's killing me!" Of course they'd find a way to feed Thunder. And water him. They could do this. They'd find a way. She kept her chin high, then suddenly lashed out. "Hey, I haven't thought all this through yet! Why are you expecting me to have all the answers right away? I mean, we just got here."

"Whoa," Griff said, pushing his palm to his white forehead. "We'll figure it out." He looked toward the loft and the small wooden steps leading up. "Think there's a nice bed of straw up there for sleeping?" he asked.

"Maybe," Libby said. "If you don't mind falling through the boards."

Griff walked closer to Thunder and rested his foot on a stall board. "Hey, Lib. Thunder's bleeding."

"Where?" She didn't move from her chair.

"Halfway up his right thigh," Griff said. "Blood's dripping. That dog must have bitten him."

Libby looked through the boards. "Jeez." Blood dripped from a nasty gash on Thunder's leg. Why hadn't she noticed it? She pulled off her right tennis shoe, then her left, which was incredibly tight. As she removed it, she nearly cried out. Then she eased off her socks and tied the ends together. "Here," she said to Griff. "Tie this around his leg . . . to get the bleeding to stop."

"But won't he . . ."

"Just act calm."

She watched Griff pat Thunder's rump, then tie the socks around his leg. "Yeah, that's good," she said. "It's a quick fix, but a vet should look at it."

"Yeah, like you're going to get a vet out here," Griff said, head cocked. "I don't mean to be negative, but . . ."

Libby couldn't answer. A vet should look at it. Or at a minimum, she needed to put an antiseptic on it to prevent infection. Vets. How was she going to get a vet to look at Thunder's wound? And who would pay? Hoof picks. Grooming equipment. Feed. There was so much she couldn't think through. Her brain was like an overloaded washing machine, clunking off-center. She smelled of horse sweat, her hands were grimy, and her hair felt dirty, clinging to the top of her head. A hot bath and sleep and no pain, that's what she wanted. She glanced down at her bare feet in the gray light. Her left foot had ballooned. Doubled in size.

"Uh, Griff," she said.

"Yeah?"

She drew a deep breath, hoping to stay strong, but it came out in a whine. Her chin trembled. "My foot hurts really bad."

"Let me take a look at it," Griff said.

Wind gusted suddenly into the barn. A voice threaded its way behind it. "Here you are."

In the grayness of the barn, it took a moment to focus on the form, but Libby knew the molasses voice instantly. She froze. Along her temple, a vein throbbed.

White shirt dirt-streaked, black hair rumpled, Porter walked steadily toward them with a fixed smile—slowly, carefully—as if with any luck, he might catch a pair of wild rabbits with his bare hands.

CHAPTER FOURTEEN

"Libby," Porter said, approaching in the dim light, "you should be ashamed."

Motionless, Libby sat on the chair. The skin around her foot felt tight, ready to burst. "I had to protect him," she said. Anger flared in her chest. "From you!"

"Protect him? Right." Porter walked closer. "A woman phoned. Saw a horse kick her dog in the teeth, asked if I knew whose horse it might be. She described you and your friend."

"But how'd you know . . ." Griff asked.

"Oh, c'mon. This property and barn . . . first place to look." He fixed a longer gaze on Griff. "Aren't you the kid they caught lighting garbage cans on fire back of Shooter's Hardware?"

Griff shook his head. "No . . . it was firecrackers, that's all. It was just for fun. I wasn't trying to start . . ." He stopped and pulled back, tucking his head in like a retreating turtle. "Besides, what do you care?"

Porter turned to Libby again. "Hang out with trouble," he said, "you get in trouble. And I thought you were a good kid, Lib."

Lib. As if he were a close friend. Libby squared her arms over her chest. "I am a good kid," she said. But what energy she had suddenly withered. She leaned forward, elbows on her knees. Thunder rumbled, leaned his head over the stall, and nudged his muzzle against the top of her head.

"And here you are," Porter said, legs planted apart, three yards in front of Libby, "with *whose* horse?" His face compressed, then he shouted, "Whose horse is this, anyway?!"

Like a kitten trapped in a sack, Libby's heart flip-flopped.

Griff stepped from the stall and stretched his arm in front of her. "You don't have to answer him. He knows."

Libby understood what Jolene had to deal with all those years. Embers of anger sparked into flame. "It's okay, Griff." She firmly moved his arm away and though her hands trembled, she looked up and met Porter's glare. "By law," she said, "*you* own him. But Thunder will never really belong to you. I'm the one who loves him. He should belong to me."

"Huh," Porter said, seemingly caught off-guard. He crossed his arms and turned on his radio voice.

"That's a good speech you've worked up, but I'm taking this horse home, then I'm pressing charges against you and this other kid—for horse theft."

"But . . ." Libby leaped to her feet—instant mistake—and crumpled to the ground. She held her left knee to her chest and let out a sharp cry.

"You're *too* much," Porter said, turning away to the stall. "You should take up acting." He unhooked the latch and grabbed Thunder. "C'mon, Thunder," he said, his voice cool and controlled. "Let's get you home where you belong." The Appaloosa snorted, but followed Porter out of the barn.

Griff hurried after them and watched from the doorway. "He's . . . jeez . . . he's making Thunder keep up with him, just holding the reins from his cab window. And he's not going very slow, either."

Libby dangled her legs on either side of Griff's bike seat. With every bump in the road, her foot throbbed. Every so often he asked, "How ya doin'?"

"Okay," she lied.

She hung on to Griff's waist as his body moved up and down over the pedals. His back grew warm and sweaty beneath his T-shirt. "Good thing for the hills— downhill, that is," he said, puffing up another incline. They reached the top, then coasted down the next hill.

At long last they passed the stable and turned into

the Rosellis' driveway. Starlings sang gratingly from the oaks, as if it were their duty to wake up Ruby and alert her. Libby slid off the bike onto her good foot. "Here," Griff said, "use my shoulder." Libby hobbled along, one hand on Griff, until she made it to her doorstep. "Thanks," she managed, then using the step railing, hopped to the top step, and slowly, slowly turned the front porch door handle.

Before stepping in, she waved good-bye.

Griff nodded, then jumped on his bike. His tires rumbled over gravel and soon grew faint and silent.

Libby eased herself into her cotton-lined sleeping bag, found the least painful position for her foot, and closed her eyes.

For the next hour, she replayed the night through her mind. If only she'd thought of another place to take Thunder, but where? Her mind drifted, in and out of half-sleep, always circling back to the unbearable pain in her foot.

As the sun climbed higher, Libby heard sounds of stirring. Sounds of Ruby filling the tea kettle with water. Before long, Ruby stepped from the living room out onto the porch. Her face was freshly made up, brighter than the morning sun spilling onto Libby's sleeping bag.

"Morning," she said. "Sorry to wake you, but I knew you'd want to know . . ."

"What?" Libby raised her head off her pillow, then

with a shiver of pain from her foot to her teeth, let out a moan. She dropped back and forced herself to be still.

"Jolene's back. Spotted her little blue car pullin' in over there just a few minutes ago."

Libby started to sit up, then laid down abruptly. "I have to talk to her."

"Well, there's always the phone," Ruby said.

The thought of getting to the kitchen phone was too much. "Say, are you okay?" Ruby squatted on broad knees beside Libby and touched her forehead with the flat of her hand, which felt cool. "Are you sick?" she asked.

"I don't know," Libby muttered, and felt tears reaching flood level.

"How about some Tylenol?" Ruby asked.

"Yeah, and an ice pack, too. In the freezer."

After Ruby examined Libby's foot, she insisted on calling her parents, who arrived within the hour. Her mother stared at Libby's swollen foot. "My gosh, Libby. How did this happen?"

"I twisted it after the bonfire," Libby said. "Fell." That was all she wanted to say. Actually, talking was hard.

By eleven, they were in Dr. Hasbro's office. The doctor poked her tiny fingers along Libby's ankle and foot bones. When she hit the mark, Libby clenched her teeth.

"Ow! That hurts!"

The doctor looked up at Libby's parents, who stood side by side as if waiting for orders. "We'll want to see X-rays," she said. A nurse rolled in a wheelchair, smiled broadly, as if showing off the extra-wide space between her front teeth, and said, "Looks like I get to take you for a ride." Libby was rolled to the X-ray lab, then returned again.

Before long, Dr. Hasbro put the black-and-white film up on the lit viewing screen. She pointed out two faint jagged lines, like lines etched in fine marble. "The good news," she said, "is your ankle's fine."

"Well, that's good," Dad said.

"The bad news," the doctor said, arms around the clipboard and pressed to her chest, "is that you fractured two foot bones."

While Libby sat on an examination table, holding her foot at a right angle, toes toward the ceiling, the doctor fit white mesh around her calf and foot, then wrapped it around and around in white gauze. "We'll put a temporary cast on today. Then later this week you'll get a permanent cast, the kind your friends can sign. Oh, and you'll need crutches. At least at first."

"Crutches? I won't be able to do anything." How was she going to check up on Thunder? Who would look out for him?

"Oh, sure you will," her mother said.

"And," the doctor continued, "you should prop up your leg—two pillows under your knee, three under your foot, keep it above heart level—for the next twenty-four hours to keep down the swelling."

"Twenty-four hours?"

CHAPTER FIFTEEN

The first thing Libby did once she got home was to
hobble into the house on her silver crutches with yellow shoulder and hand pads, and get to the phone.
Why had she once thought crutches would be fun?
They were extremely hard work. She leaned them
against the wall, pushed two stools toward the glass
windows, then grabbed the phone. She sat on the stool.
Her foot wasn't elevated above her heart with pillows
under it, but she'd do that after she spoke with Jolene.

She dialed and looked out the sliding glass doors.
Beyond the rows of green-leafed trees, fence and pasture, Jolene's car glinted like a sapphire in the Porters'
driveway. God, don't let Mr. Porter answer, please. It
rang once, twice, three times, four.

"Hello?" came Jolene's voice. She sounded distant,
more of an acquaintance than a friend.

"Jolene?" Libby said. "It's me ... hi. I just ..."

"Oh, Libby, hi. Nice to hear your voice."

"Yeah, well, Ruby saw your car." She tried to smile. "Said you were home."

There was a pause. "Bet you think I'm kind of silly writing that note . . ." Jolene said, adding a light laugh that lacked sparkle. "But I'm back to stay."

"So," Libby said, "I was wondering . . . I can't today, but tomorrow . . . can I come over?"

There was silence.

Libby wondered if Jolene hadn't heard. "Could I come over tomorrow?"

Suddenly, the phone was muffled, but Libby could hear conversation:

"Who is it?" asked Mr. Porter.

"Just Libby."

"I'm sick of that kid always hanging around here. Tell her no. Jeez. You don't need her help anymore. Can't we have some privacy for a change?"

Jolene came back on the line. "Uh, hi," Jolene said. "Sorry to keep you waiting. You know, Jim and I probably need some time alone for a bit. We're working on things. So better if we wait awhile before you come over."

"Wait? Like . . . um . . . how long?"

"Um . . . oh, maybe a few weeks, perhaps."

"Maybe never," came Mr. Porter's voice, followed by a snort-laugh.

"I miss our rides, too, Libby," Jolene said softly, warmly. "Thanks so much for calling."

"But . . ."

"Listen, I have to . . ."

Suddenly, the phone slammed in Libby's ear. Libby held the phone, the dial tone buzzing, and studied its glowing push buttons. It wasn't like Jolene to hang up like that. It had to have been her husband. And weeks? She wasn't going to be allowed to go over to see Thunder? Her heart took a sharp turn. She chewed at the corner of her mouth and gazed out toward the Porter's property. Suddenly there was movement. Libby squinted.

From the house, Jolene emerged—her red hair bright, even from a distance—and hurried to her sapphire car, Porter walking after her. She hopped in, then sped down the driveway toward the road. Dust swirled up behind, trailing her like a cloud. In the car's wake, Porter stood like a store mannequin. Just stood there, watching his wife leave. Things, it seemed, weren't going so well. After a few long moments, Porter turned away and walked toward the barn. Libby winced and hoped Thunder was out to pasture. Quickly she scanned the fields, but didn't see him. From her stool, she wasn't seeing the complete pasture. The horses could be on the far side of the barn, too. She made a vow: She'd keep her leg propped up all day, but swelling or not, she was heading back to the barn. Soon.

When Libby's mother stepped in from outside, she

said, "Libby, let's just set you up on the front porch. Avoid going up and down those stairs, okay?"

Her mother helped get pillows under her leg, hoisting her foot high. Though it still hurt to move it, the medicine at least took the edge off the pain. Before heading out again, her mother handed Libby her portable phone. "When the phone rings," she said, "you won't have to get up." She turned to the porch door, then stopped. Sunlight refracted off the second earring—a small diamond—in her mother's right ear. "Oh, and one more thing . . ."

Libby pushed strands of hair from her face. She suddenly was exhausted.

"Jim Porter called earlier. And, well . . . he said you've been over there late at night—after midnight. Is this true?" Her eyes reminded Libby of mink coats, deep brown with a touch of red.

Libby nodded.

"I know you miss the horses, Libby, but that's no excuse for sneaking out like that. . . ." She pressed her forefinger to her lips, paused, inhaled hard, then continued. "And he also shared his concern that you've, well, been hanging around with a boy who's been in some trouble. Lives with the Wheelers now, apparently. Jim said he didn't want to go into detail, but he was concerned about you . . . this boy's influence on you . . ."

Libby's stomach felt squeamish. She felt she was

being pressed into a dark corner, only she couldn't see or feel its boundaries.

"I went over to see Thunder, Mom. That part's true, but Porter's wrong about Griff. He's nice, he really is."

"Well, time will tell on that," Mom said, "but for now..." She cast a glance at Libby's foot. "For twenty-four hours, you're grounded." And then she laughed and the right corner of her mouth lifted in a smile. "As if you have much choice, right?"

Libby didn't smile. "Right."

Her mother headed outside.

Within seconds, Libby picked the phone off the floor and dialed Griff's number. Her chest tightened, and her heart pulsed, but not quite as hard as with the first call.

"Yeah?" Griff said, answering. "I mean, Wheelers'. Griff speaking."

"Hi," Libby said.

"Hey ... how's it going?"

"I broke my foot," she said, studying her odd appendage. "It's in a temporary cast."

"You're kidding, right?"

She shook her head, then answered. "No, honest, I did. Fractured two bones. I have to get around on crutches," she said, "but that won't stop us from going back to the stable tonight, right?"

"Tonight?"

"Yup."

"Are you sure?"

"Positive."

"Are you crazy?"

Libby paused, flashed on Thunder's beautiful spotted blanket, the way he tossed his head trotting toward her in the moonlight, his gentle eyes—one tinged red.

"Probably."

CHAPTER SIXTEEN

At three minutes past midnight, Griff showed. After
napping the whole afternoon, Libby was wide awake.
Griff held the porch door open for her. She maneuvered
out and down the steps on her crutches. "If we get
caught again . . ." Griff whispered.

Libby shook her head. "We're *not* getting caught this
time." Her foot began to throb, but now that it was held
firm with the temporary cast and she was on painkillers,
it felt much better. She step-hopped across the yard.
Griff walked alongside in slow motion. At the white
fence, Libby stopped. "Good. His truck's gone." She
whistled once and waited. No horses responded, so after
what seemed like hours, they crossed the pasture and
arrived at the barn door.

Griff opened the swinging door and Libby hobbled
ahead. Then, from behind, he clicked on a flashlight
beam. Mitts darted through the beam, then disappeared
along the barn floor.

"Hi, Mitts," Libby whispered. Barn cats, they had a mind of their own.

The horses stirred in their stalls. Jolene must be gone again—for good. If she were back in charge, the horses would be out grazing in the cooler night air, without flies thick on their bodies.

Like a ghost in the darkness, Cincinnati hung her white head over her stall. She whinnied softly.

"Shhhh," Libby said. With her shoulders resting into the arm pads, she stroked the mare's fine cheekbones. Two-Step, in the next stall, lifted his head up and down. Libby hobbled to him. "Hi, boy," she said, and patted the flat of his nose.

Across from the other two horses, Thunder rose to his legs in his stall and shook his coat. He stretched over his gate and pressed his muzzle toward Libby's shorts pocket.

"I'll get you a treat," she whispered. She hadn't remembered to bring sugar cubes. But Jolene always kept a box of apple treats—red apple-shaped biscuits that the horses loved—on a tack room shelf. They'd do.

Like a shadow, Griff followed Libby to the tack room. She shined the beam around the leather equipment, the neat piles of stable pamphlets and papers on Jolene's desk.

"Lots of stuff," Griff said.

"She always keeps it organized. Everything in its place. That's Jolene."

On a middle shelf, Libby found the treats and grabbed a handful from the box.

Truck tires grumbled in the gravel driveway.

Libby froze. Like soapy water swirling down a drain, her courage vanished.

"Uh-oh," Griff whispered. He clicked off the flashlight.

The vehicle's door slammed shut, followed by a clank.

Libby tried to think. They had to hide. Maybe under the desk, but it wouldn't be easy to scramble to her knees. And she couldn't hide the crutches. "Thunder's stall," she said. "C'mon."

Griff followed her, then unbolted the stall door. Libby clunked in. Thunder danced nervously. If Porter was planning to hurt Thunder, he'd have to deal with them first.

Libby's crutches sank deep in cedar chips. She leaned against the stall's wall. Griff crouched down and peered through the stall slats. For a moment or two it was silent, then the stable door slid open.

Libby inched her head out, just far enough to see. Framed in the opening, silhouetted by the moonlit yard, was Mr. Porter. In his right hand, he lugged a small can with a spigot. He looked over his shoulder toward the dark house, then back into the barn.

He moved toward the hay bales just inside the door, leaned forward and poured from the can. The smell of fresh gasoline wafted to Libby's nose. She started to edge to the stall door. Griff clamped her arm.

Mr. Porter stepped back into the stable's doorway, flinging something toward the bales. "Stupid matches," he muttered.

Libby watched blankly, then in a flash, understood. She unbolted Thunder's stall, heart pounding in her chest, and pushed out through the stall door. The same second the match lit. The next moment the small flame hit the pool of gasoline and roared into a ball of curling hot fire above the bales.

Back-pedaling quickly, Porter stared at the fire, then quickly shoved the door closed and was gone.

In their stalls, the horses snorted and danced.

The orange ball of fire sent out runners to crossbeams.

"The horses!" Libby yelled, turning away, her body flooding with adrenaline. Three horses. Two people. One on crutches. Why did Porter set his own barn on fire? The answer hit her gut like lead: money. Insurance money. They had to get the horses out.

She hobbled in circles, then stopped. Calm down, she told herself. Think. Think. Griff stood only three feet away, his blond hair bright in the illuminated light. He blinked, as if hypnotized by the fire.

"Griff, open their stall doors," Libby said.

Libby step-hopped to the tack room, grabbed bridles, and draped them over her shoulder. Then she made her way back out. Step-hop. Step-hop. Though his stall door was open, Thunder hadn't fled. "Get outta here!" Libby cried, stepping in. Thunder spun away from her, his eyes white, then reared, black hoofs glinting in the bright glow of firelight. Avoiding his pummeling hooves, Libby stepped to his side and reached up, glad he was wearing his halter.

"C'mon boy!" she pleaded. "Please!" She pulled harder on his halter. But the harder she pulled, the more he resisted, throwing his head back in defiance, nostrils flared pink. He pushed back deeper into the stall. He flinched, but still refused to step forward, just the way he'd refused to cross the Bancroft wooden bridge: that time, she'd tied a windbreaker around Thunder's head, covered his eyes, and led him across.

"No!" Libby shouted. What had Jolene said? *Don't pull—you'll never win. Get alongside and walk with him.*

Libby leaned her crutches against the stall wall, hopped to Thunder's side, and balancing on her good foot, flung his bridle over his neck. With her thumb inside the corner of his mouth, she slid the bit inside. Then she grabbed his reins, hopped with him to the edge of the stall, crawled up a few boards, and hoisted herself up and over across his back. She reached down and pushed open his stall door. He pranced sideways, and her foot bumped against the door frame. Pain spiked through her, but she ignored it.

She forced her voice lower, calmer. "Thunder, it's okay, Thunder," she said, her heart thudding. In the center of the barn, smoke hung in a dark mass. Libby's eyes stung. She clicked her tongue and covered her mouth and nose with her hand. Atop Thunder, Libby spotted Griff outside Cincinnati's stall.

"What do I do?" he called. "They won't leave their stalls!"

Libby reined Thunder back toward the tack room, reached in around the corner, and grabbed two saddle blankets from a high shelf. Then she rode Thunder back toward Griff. "Here. Get it around her head," she said, handing him the blankets, "then I'll lead her out."

"I'll try." He dropped the extra blanket outside the stall, then stepped into where Cincinnati was pressed in the corner, nickering.

Hungry flames arced up toward the rafters, snapping. How could the fire spread so quickly? The gasoline had created an explosion of fire. It fed on the hay bales and the bin of cedar chips alongside the bales.

"Touch her neck first," Libby coached. "Then slide the blanket up and over her head."

The mare inched sideways from the blanket. "I can't—she won't hold still!" But in seconds, Griff had the blanket around her head, her eyes covered. He walked her out of her stall, his hand beneath the gathered blanket. "Got her?" he asked, as Libby reached over to the mare's head.

"Got her," she said.

"Okay, one left," Griff said, and headed to the next stall, blanket in hand.

Libby stretched over to hold onto Cincinnati, grasping the edges of the blanket beneath the mare's small head.

Behind her, something crashed to the ground. Libby glanced back. The antique snow sled that had hung by twine to the rafters had fallen to the barn's floor. She pushed forward, barely able to make out the pasture door. Straight line. Just head for it, she told herself. Don't get turned around. Every second counts.

Acrid smoke burned her lungs.

Thunderbird lunged left, then right, but Libby held on and nudged him with her knees toward the door. If only it were open. She pulled back on Thunder's reins, let the mare take a few steps forward, then quickly urged Thunder forward, nudging his chest into the mare's rump. She balked, but lunged, and the door swung open. The blanket fell from Cincinnati's head and she galloped out into the pasture.

They were out. She gulped air. She rode Thunder farther from the barn, then stopped him and looked back.

Smoke spilled black out the door. Beyond it, inside, flames pulsed.

"Oh, no," Libby said, covering her mouth with her hand. Where were Griff and Two-Step?

Suddenly, Two-Step, head blanketed, shot out the door, his dark coat slick in firelight, with Griff stumbling alongside. He pulled the horse blanket off Two-Step's head, and the horse danced in a semicircle as Griff held the bay by the rope. "I did it!"

There was something else. Libby racked her mind, staring at the fire. It spat and groaned like a living thing. "Oh, no," she said. "Mitts!"

Griff looked up at Libby.

Roaring filled the barn. A whoosh of heat forced them yards back. Flames lapped at the edges of the door, then curled toward the roof. Libby's mouth hung slack. Her face burned. She edged back farther and farther, away from the scalding heat. Her chest filled with an ache. Mitts was inside.

CHAPTER SEVENTEEN

From the barn, a crash sounded. An ember rocketed from the upper window and landed near Griff's feet. The breeze licked it into flames. He stomped it out, still hanging on to Two-Step's lead rope. The bay snorted, his nostrils flaring wide, and backed away, dragging Griff along, then stopped.

On Thunder's back, Libby remembered the bridles dangling from the crook of her elbow. She nudged Thunder closer to Two-Step, reached over awkwardly, and tried to bridle the quarter horse. Two-Step backed away. "Hold him," she told Griff. She managed to curve her right arm over the top of Two-Step's neck, slide her left thumb into the back of his mouth so he'd open it, then deftly slip in the bit. She had thought she'd grabbed another bridle, but her hands were empty now.

"Griff," she said. "Unclip the lead rope, and hand it to me."

He reached under the bay's chin, then handed Libby the rope.

"Now hop up on him. I'll get Cincinnati, and we'll get these horses out of here."

"But I've only gone on pony rides," he moaned.

"Just jump up."

"How?"

"The fence rail there," she said, pointing to the furthest edge of the paddock. Behind her, the barn wheezed. A crackling roar filled her ears. "Get up on his left side. And hurry!"

Halterless, Cincinnati had ambled farther into the pasture. Libby trotted Thunder beside the mare, looped the lead rope through its steel clip, and wrapped the rope around Cincinnati's neck. Hot air pressed against Libby's back. Thunder snorted and danced. "It's okay, fella. We'll get away from here."

Shaking, she took hold of Thunder's reins in her left hand and Cincinnati's rope in her right, then pressed her knees into Thunder's sides. He bolted. As one, the three horses cantered across the pasture.

"Oh, sheezh!" Griff cried, hanging on to Two-Step's neck.

Like wild mustangs, the horses raced past the clustered oaks to the far end of the pasture. Just when it seemed they might crash through the fence, Thunderbird drew his haunches beneath him and stopped at the corner gate, tossing his head.

Griff, half on and half off, clung like a sticky noodle to Two-Step's neck. "I'm gonna get killed!" he cried, managing to sit up and center himself.

They looked back. Flames shot from the ends of the barn, winding to meet in a handshake along the roof at the horse weathervane and sparking the dark sky.

"I can't believe . . ." she began, but didn't finish. The smell of smoke clung to her hair, rose from her lungs with each deep breath. Unable to shake the image of Mr. Porter striking the match, Libby leaned down across Thunder's shoulder to the gate. Fingers trembling, she fumbled the latch, pushed open the gate with her left foot, and nudged Thunder out, holding the door wide for the others to follow. It swung shut behind them.

Amidst patches of moonlight, the horses trotted, the mare alongside Thunder, and Two-Step behind, along the well-trod trail through the woods. A branch scraped Libby's cheek, then sprang back again as she passed. "Branch," she called behind her.

"Ouch!" Griff moaned.

They rode around the north side of the pasture, on the outside of the fence, circling back toward the willows. Like a giant bonfire, the barn lit up the sky. Libby's heart pounded. "We have to get them away from him!"

"Got that right."

Libby swallowed her anger. "The ravine. We'll take them there." Her stomach tightened. "We can swim them across the river to Wisconsin. Get them as far away as possible."

As they neared the pond, the barn blazed higher. "Whoa," Libby said. The horses clustered in the dark fringe beyond the fire's far-reaching circle of light.

"What if Porter spots us?" Griff asked, his knee lightly touching hers.

"I don't see his truck," she answered. "He must have lit the barn and taken off."

Flames danced through the air, arcing from the stable to the Porters' house and fingering its shingles. The fire grew louder, crackling, refusing to be tamed.

Within seconds, sirens whined from the south.

Cincinnati reared, but Libby held her rope. "Easy, girl. Easy."

Careening around the corner into the Porters' driveway, a fire engine rolled in, its orange light glowing. Two police cars followed. The sirens stopped, and the fire's roar seemed to grow louder still, as if it were a defiant dragon, spewing fire and at the same time sucking everything consumable toward its mouth. Like frenzied ants, yellow-clad firefighters poured from the truck, headgear on. They moved quickly, grabbing hoses, carrying axes, running toward the stable and house. They hooked up wide hoses and blasted the fire with water.

Thunder whipped his tail, slapping at Libby's leg.

"Let's go while they're focused on the fire," Griff whispered.

Firefighters scurried, turning their full attention to the barn, to the smoke and flames pouring from the roof's edges. Smoke-filled wind rushed through the willow leaves.

Suddenly, as if kicked by a horse, it struck Libby; if they hadn't been there, the horses would have died. No amount of kicking or whinnying would have helped them. Images filled her mind. If she and Griff hadn't been there, Thunder would already be dead. She shivered involuntarily and clenched her jaw. She didn't care what the laws were, or who legally owned Thunder. She was never taking him back. Laying the reins alongside Thunder's neck, she turned the Appaloosa around. She firmly held Cincinnati's rope and led the way from the pond toward the road. The horses' hooves clomped across the pavement, then grew silent as they followed the path down the grassy slope, found a narrow path, and headed into the ravine.

Thunder braced his legs against the incline, but started down. Down the steep, thickly rooted path, a few miles of twists and turns, alongside steep grooves, toward Highway 61 and the Mississippi River snaking below. "It's okay, Thunder," Libby whispered.

A light clicked on from behind her, illuminating Libby's bare thigh. "Would this help?" Griff asked, holding the flashlight, riding last behind Cincinnati, whose head nearly rested on Thunder's spotted rump.

"I figured you left it in the barn," Libby said. She was trusting Thunder to stay on the trail, since he knew it. But his hooves kept slipping—*thwuck, thwuck*—in muddy patches left from the morning's rain. Libby's shoulders rose and fell. Her foot hurt—needed to be propped up. But that was the last of her worries.

"Here," Griff said.

Libby reined Thunder in and reached back for the flashlight. Just as she did, she dropped Cincinnati's rope. Behind and above them, along the road, another siren whined. The mare suddenly reared, tossed her head, and pushed past Thunder. She bolted deeper into the ravine.

"Oh, great," Libby cried. She clasped the reins in her left hand and aimed the flashlight on the path. Thunder's muscles tensed. But under these conditions, she wasn't about to let him run. A horse could break its leg. "Walk," Libby said, and Thunder resumed his earlier pace.

"Where will she go?" Griff asked.

"I don't know. She's like that. Hopefully not far." Libby remembered something Jolene had said. "Arabians are like cats," Libby said out loud, "they have their own ideas about things."

Ferns and moss carpeted portions of the trail. Old

stands of leafy maple and basswood shrouded their way. Roots crept like thick snakes, intertwining and knotting. Thunder picked his way carefully through the thickest masses. At one point, a windblown tree blocked the trail. Libby nudged Thunder wide around it, pushing through raspberry nettles and underbrush, then swung the flashlight back and forth, searching for the trail again. She found it.

They rode for an endless time, hunched over the horses' necks, so as to not get swiped off by an unexpected branch.

"So where'd she go?" Griff asked.

Libby shrugged. "I wish I knew." They were far enough away now, deep in the belly of the ravine. Libby called for the mare. She whistled. But there was no response. Wind played in the leaves, carrying with it the smell of smoke. Again they moved on.

A tabby cat, scraggly coated with one ear tattered, appeared in the flashlight's beam. It shot an eerie yellow-eyed stare their way, then slunk off, its belly low to the ground. It made Libby think of Mitts. Mitts, who had carefully given her kittens baths, had faithfully licked them head to toe. She sighed heavily.

Twice Thunder stopped, but Libby urged him on with the click of her tongue. They had no choice but to go forward. She blinked back fatigue, focused on seeing straight ahead, and kept going.

In small gullies along their trail, water wound its

way down—down to a creek, a wider stream, and on toward the Mississippi below. Water flows to the point of least resistance. Someone said that.

A rushing sound came from ahead, water rushing over rocks and sand, cascading in small steps downward. The creek. The creek with no bridge. They'd have to walk across it. It was too wide to jump. At its edge, Libby shone the light on the water. Thunder complained with short snorts and tossed his brown mane.

Not far beyond the creek, the trail crossed the highway. A busy highway. She didn't want the mare to get that far.

Suddenly, from somewhere through the green trees and undergrowth, came the sickening screech of brakes, of crunching metal. Libby's heart sank. "Oh, no!" she cried, and lifted Thunder's reins. "C'mon, let's go."

Thunder slid down the creek's bank, splashed across in uneasy lurches through the knee-deep water, then bolted up the other side.

"Whoa, mama!" came Griff's voice and Two-Step's harder breathing from behind. "If this keeps up," he said, "I'm never going to be a father!"

Libby ignored his comment. She dreaded what might be ahead. She let Thunder canter the rest of the way down the trail, which widened and widened, first to a grassy rest area with scattered picnic tables, then to a small parking lot. And beneath a single streetlamp, beside the sloping highway, only a five-minute ride to the river which glittered below, was the Golden Wheat Bakery truck, its front end smashed against the base of a bluff.

And in the road beyond the truck, lying on her side, lay Cincinnati.

Perfectly white, perfectly still.

CHAPTER EIGHTEEN

Yards off, Libby stopped Thunder.

Griff rode up beside her. "What the. . . ?"

A dull, cold ache settled in Libby's chest. She wished this were a dream. But she knew otherwise. The flashlight dropped from her hand to the ground, and Thunder flinched, his muscles moving like waves beneath Libby's legs. She brought her hand to her mouth.

Reluctantly, she urged Thunder closer. He stepped, turning his head to eye the still white form. He lowered his head to the mare's muzzle, sniffed, and with his nostrils flaring, jerked back.

Libby fell into Thunder's neck and pressed her cheek against his warm coat.

"Hey! Get me outta here!" came a muffled voice from the truck. Libby jumped. She'd forgotten the truck had a driver. The front end was smashed in so deeply, it was a wonder anyone could be alive at all.

She clicked her tongue and nudged Thunder around to the driver's window, right up to the concave door. Mr. Freeman, the father of one of her classmates, his forehead bloody, knocked on the window. "Can't move my legs or get this door open! I called for help." From inside the delivery truck, voices buzzed on a CB radio.

Just then, a police car rounded the bend and parked in the center of the road, lights flashing. Doors flung open. The officers ran toward the truck. "Radio in," the woman officer called over her shoulder and pulled at the truck door. "We're going to need some more help here."

Libby trotted Thunder away from the truck, back into the shadows near the picnic tables. The sky was turning pale gray. Birds began to sing—a predawn chorus.

The woman officer was at the other side of the truck, opening the door. "How 'ya doin' in there?" she asked, climbing in.

"Sooner I get outta here, the better," came Mr. Freeman's reply. "This ain't no picnic."

Swaying his bulky form in question over the horse, the other officer called over his shoulder, "This horse is deader than a doornail."

Then he looked up, past the mare, and saw Libby and Griff staring back at him. "What are you two . . ." He looked back at the mare, and scanned the ground.

His tone grew more serious. "Was there another rider here?"

Libby shook her head. "No," she said lamely. "We were only trying to save them."

"Them?"

"The horses."

"Bad night for horses," the officer said. "Porter's barn just burned to the ground with a few horses inside." Then he seemed to study Griff, who was appearing to study his left knee or an ant on the ground. "Wait. You're maybe . . . what's your name, kid?"

Griff's eyes met Libby's. Between nearly closed lips, he breathed, "What d'we do? Take off for the river?"

The officer studied Libby's face. "And you. You're a Roselli."

Libby recognized the officer's extra-thick white eyebrows under his cap. She knew him. Though he wasn't often at the stable, he came in a few times every summer to get apples. He was Jolene's father. "You two stay put," he said. "Second thought, one of you can wait with the horses." With a swirl of his forefinger, he motioned to Griff. "Slide down there and come with me. I'm making a few calls, and I've got a few questions—for both of you."

Griff groaned, slid off Two-Step's back, and handed Libby the reins. "We're in trouble now," he said.

He looked up at Libby and gave her a quick salute. With a slight swagger, blond hair bobbing, he followed the officer to the police car. Casual. Cool. As if it were no big deal. The officer motioned to the back—Griff climbed in—and the officer climbed in the front, then pressed a receiver to his mouth.

Libby turned her gaze back to Cincinnati, and stared. It almost seemed that at any moment the mare would stir, rise to her legs and take off again. Libby's body and brain felt rubbery, numb. Her breathing grew fast and shallow. She wanted the whole thing, like a bad dream, to stop.

Within minutes, brakes squeaking, a small car pulled up behind the squad car. Jolene sprang from her car, hair loose around the shoulders of her white tank top, and ran past the side of the bread truck. She fell to her knees beside Cincinnati's head. "Poor baby . . ." she cried. "Poor girl." Slowly, she ran her hands along the horse's side, then stroked the mare's cheek. Finally, slowly, she rose, head bowed over the Arabian. She looked up at Libby. "I just came from the stable. Jim said the horses were inside—all dead. Now my dad calls me to come here. And here you are. Cincinnati's"—her voice cracked—"dead. None of this makes . . . makes any sense."

"I feel so bad," Libby whispered, wishing the mare would breathe, move, anything but lie so abnormally still. Her face crumpled. "I tried to save her."

Another police car rolled in. This time, Mr. Porter jumped from the passenger side. He spotted Libby, then eyed Griff in the backseat of the other squad car. "Well, that was quick," he bellowed. "Caught the little sucker!" He glanced from the young policeman to Libby. "Told you to be careful who you hang out with, Lib. Sorry to learn you got caught up in this mess."

"What?"

Porter walked calmly to Libby's side and swiped a sideways glance at the downed mare. "I told the police about you stealing the horse yesterday. Now that they learned more about your friend, well, it's pretty obvious." He snapped a glance back at the first police car, where Griff still waited. "Seems your friend started the barn on fire. Got a call at Jack's Place and came back home to see it like a damn torch." He put his hands to his hips. "Thought the horses were killed, but I see you *stole* them." Porter grabbed Thunder's reins close beneath the bit and met her eyes. "Again."

Inside Libby a volcano grew and climbed to its edges. "First, I didn't start the fire," she said. "You did. If I took the horses, it was only to protect them from *you!*"

The youngest officer stepped into the circle, studied Libby, and shifted his feet.

"See?" Porter said to the officer. "This is what I told you she'd say. She's desperate," he said, shaking his head sympathetically. "It's okay, Libby. Don't worry. Nobody will be too hard on you. Things are gonna work out."

A rush of emotion rose to her eyes, but Libby bit her lip. She wasn't going to cry—not now—and plunged ahead. "I'm . . . telling . . . the truth! You started the fire yourself. Griff and I—we both saw you!"

Porter pressed both hands flat toward her, as if holding back traffic. "Now, wait a holy second there. You're making accusations you can't possibly prove."

"If we hadn't been there to get the horses out, they all would have been killed—and you know it!"

Thunder pawed.

Jolene's father—the older officer—was suddenly at Porter's elbow. Jolene walked closer, arms tight across her chest. She looked from Libby to Porter to her father. "Dad," she said, her voice pained. "Twice before, Jim said that we'd be better off if the whole barn burned down."

"Joking," Porter snapped. "You don't think I'd actually do something that stupid, do you?" He reached for his wife's shoulder, but Jolene slipped from his grasp.

A V etched itself in her forehead and she raised her voice. "He said that money would be more useful than a barnful of horses." She paused, her face tight. Her chin trembled. "I know Libby—and I believe her. Every word. The only thing that appears to be an accident tonight," she said, tilting her chin toward the mare, "is this. And what a *waste* of a beautiful animal."

"Hey, I was at Jack's," Porter said to the officers. "You just ask 'em down there." Panic crept into his face and settled in his eyes. He looked to Libby. "You tell them . . . you wanted Thunder, right . . . and . . ."

Libby looked away.

Porter swore. "What a mess."

Jolene's father's eyebrows rose up, then lowered. "Okay, let's not go any further with this here. We're going to need to get statements, so whatever else anyone wants to say can keep until we get back to the station, got it?"

CHAPTER NINETEEN

Libby rode Thunder, and Griff—who refused to sit for at least a week—walked alongside, leading Two-Step. In the early morning light, his face was smudged gray, his hair dulled to ash blond, but his eyes were blue as the sky. "Guess when it comes to riding, I'm a wimp, huh?" he asked, looking up.

"No," Libby said, "you're not a wimp. I mean, you got Two-Step out of the barn. You rode him and didn't even fall off."

"Yeah, that wasn't bad, huh?"

Libby smiled at him.

The horses' hooves beat a soft, steady rhythm on the damp shoulder. At the top of a hill, sunlight hit Libby's face. She shaded her eyes with her hand. In the distance, the Mississippi wound like a silver snake between wetlands, sandbars, and tiny islands.

They passed the Porters' driveway. The wooden Northwind Stables sign lay busted in half; apparently the fire engine hadn't cleared under it. Beyond it, the barn was merely charred spindles rising above the ground. Nothing was left. And without the barn, the pasture had a wide gap in its fencing. For now, they'd have to bring the horses to Libby's and tie them up outside. Something caught her eye.

Slinking through the grass, Mitts suddenly pounced, trapped an object between her white paws, then darted with it under the low, sweeping branches of the blue spruce.

"Oh—," Libby said with a sigh. "She made it!" She wished the same were true of Cincinnati. Why did the little mare have to run off and get hit? It still didn't seem possible that she was dead. Libby swallowed hard, her throat tight. She'd never forget her.

In silence, they rode to Libby's driveway. A pigeon pecked in the gravel, then flapped into the oak branches. Her parents' vehicle was parked beside Ruby's blue Plymouth. Libby rode Thunder straight up to the house.

"Hey!" she called. "Mom? Dad? Anybody home?"

Her parents came through the front door. Mom tilted her head sideways, looking like she might cry. "Finally," she burst out. "We've been just frantic since we heard, but the police said to stay here until you returned."

"They called a while ago, though," Dad added. "Filled us in and said you were on your way." He shook his head. "From the sounds of it—and the way you two look—you've been through . . ."

"A lot," Griff said, patting Two-Step's shoulder and looking into the bay's dark eyes. "Isn't that right, pal?"

Mom flashed a quizzical look at Griff, then stepped toward Thunder. She reached up and touched Libby's arm. "Will you get down," she whispered, "so I can give you a hug?"

Libby smiled. "Sure," she said, "If you can get me another pair of crutches."

By midday, the horses were back to their own pasture. Jolene, Libby's dad, and Griff worked together to put up temporary fencing where the barn and adjoining fence boards had burned away. Libby watched from crutches, another rented pair from the drugstore.

By late August, Libby had shed her crutches. In a knee-high purple walking cast, she hobbled along the downtown sidewalk, a black permanent ink marker in her top bib pocket. Mom parked at the library, got out, and said, "I'll meet you back here in an hour then?"

Libby nodded. "Yup."

She had arranged to meet Griff at the Apple Muffin Cafe, a green-and-white house off Main Street that had been turned into a tiny restaurant. She walked half a block and passed a garden bright with red, orange, and purple zinnias. She'd spent the night with Emily and Rachel, eating popcorn and watching movies. It hadn't been great. She couldn't tell which, but either they'd changed or she had. And that was okay. They signed her cast, right beside Griff's name. And for once, they actually listened to what she had to tell them—especially about the fire and Griff and how Porter might have to serve a few months of jail time.

Libby walked up the steps to the restaurant. Grabbing a piece of pie or a Coke together wasn't exactly a date, but still, her heart started to speed up. She turned the handle of the paned door, stepped in, and saw Griff. He was sitting at a corner table on the front porch, framed by a bookcase of books, and was wearing a black top hat. He stood up, swept the hat off his head toward the ground, and bowed. "A pleasure," he said in the tone of an elderly gentleman. But when Libby noticed his denim shorts and skinned knee, she couldn't play along. She cracked up laughing.

Two women at the porch's far table looked her way, paused from their discussion, and smiled. Griff stood on tiptoe and placed the hat back on the top shelf of the bookcase.

Jolene came out of the main dining area, her hair in tendrils around her face. Dark circles skimmed her eyes, but she smiled broadly. "Oh, my two favorite people," she said, and set down green placemats and glasses of ice water. "What can I get you?"

Libby ordered "Grandma's Own Apple Pie," à la mode. And Griff ordered a cherry Coke float. When Jolene had a free moment, she returned. In shorts and sandals, she placed one hand over her hip and white apron. "Libby," she said. "I finally found an owner for Thunder."

Libby's stomach fell three notches. It wasn't that she had thought he could ever be hers—not really—but the more days that went by without someone wanting to buy him, the more days she had to ride him. To simply enjoy him. And with the Porters splitting and selling their property to a developer, it was only until the end of summer, anyway, before heavy equipment would come in and plow up the fields in five-acre plots for new houses. "Guess it's called progress," her father had said, "but I sure hate to see the land chopped up like that."

"I took less for him than I'd first wanted," Jolene continued. She glanced at the nearby table, chewed on the end of her pen, and looked back at Libby. "But his new owners will be perfect for him. I mean, they just adore him. And they're going to let me board Two-Step there. That way I can still go riding, and Thunder will have another horse for company."

Libby swallowed and nodded her head. "That's good," she said, but her voice was an unconvincing whisper.

Jolene drew closer, squatted beside Libby's chair,

and put her arm around Libby's shoulder. "Sometime you and I could ride Two-Step together."

"And Lib," Griff said. "There's a stable, y'know, about ten miles out of LaCrosse. Maybe we could ride over there." He tapped the toes of her right foot with the toe of his boot. "If you want."

Libby thought of going for regular trail rides. Slap down your money for the hour. Get on a horse, probably a fine horse, but one you didn't really know. Clunk along, trot a few times, maybe canter once if the trail guide was feeling really generous, and then head back to the stable again. "Yeah," she said, trying to smile. "Sure."

Jolene squeezed Libby's shoulder and stood. "They picked the horses up today," she said softly. "Just as soon as it works out, I'll call." Then she headed into the main dining room.

Griff lifted his empty glass and straw to his lips.

Libby checked her watch. The hour had flown by. "Better go." They each left money on the table, got up, and headed out the door. "Stop by sometime," she said to Griff, who grabbed his bike from the side of the building.

"When do you get your cast off?" he asked.

"Two weeks—maybe four," she said. "It's killing me not to be able to swim or even bike. But I guess I'll survive." Then she headed back toward the library, found her mother inside, and caught a ride home.

"You look sad," her mother said. Her window was rolled down and moist summer air spilled in, lifting her dark hair in tiny spikes as she drove.

Libby nodded, but didn't answer. She gazed out her open window. Houses and neighborhoods blended into new developments, into farmlands and orchards. Swallows swooped down into the grassy ditch, then up over telephone lines. Graceful, unfettered. Libby swooped her hand up and down outside the car window, felt the wind's pressure against her skin. She'd never had a chance to say good-bye to Thunder, or Two-Step. Maybe it was better that way. Still, there was a chance of seeing them again. Of course, it would all be different. She was glad they'd been in her life. Cincinnati, too. Memories, at least, were something no one could ever take away.

At her driveway, the car rolled in slowly. Libby let out her breath, trying to loosen the tightness building in her chest. First thing, she'd go to her room and have a good cry. Sometimes it was the only thing to do. Then she looked up.

A red horse trailer was parked outside the Apple Shed. The Northwind Stables horse trailer. Libby held her breath. The possibility flashed through her like lightning, but she dared not believe it.

"Well, what do you know," her mother said, pulling up beside it, shifting into park, and turning the key off in the ignition. From the other side of the trailer, her father stepped out with a smile bigger than the moon itself.

Libby flew out of the car and hobbled as fast as her legs would take her to the back of the trailer. Two horse tails swished back and forth over the half-door. One rump was a sleek dark brown, the other one was spotted brown on white, a beautiful Appaloosa.

"Thunder?" she said, her voice squeaky. He turned his head toward her voice and nickered low in his usual greeting. She glanced at Dad. "But . . . I thought someone bought . . . we couldn't afford . . ."

"Well, it appears there's a reward for reporting arson with your name on it," he said. "That—and your mom and I dug a little into our savings. Things work out."

Libby studied her father's teasing smile, then tears rose to her eyes. She opened the back gate, flipped down the ramp, then hurried to the front of the trailer. She slipped in through the side door and backed each horse out, one at a time, lead ropes clamped to their halters. She walked the horses to the grass near the oaks.

Griff suddenly wheeled in on his bike. "Hey, what do you know?" He straddled the bar and winked at Libby, then smiled at her parents.

"You knew!" she nearly screamed. "Here, hold Two-Step for me."

"You bet," he said, dropping his bike to the

ground. "Jolene thought you might need an extra hand till she got off work."

Her parents stood side by side, smug as contented cats.

Libby stroked Thunder's shoulder, studied his brown socks, gentle eyes, and spotted blanket. In a whisper, as if a full voice might shatter everything, she asked, "Does this mean . . . he's really . . . ?"

She stopped. Day by day, she'd earn the right to be his owner. She'd brush him daily, make sure he got regular exercise, and always supply him with good feed and clean water. She'd learn to listen to what he was trying to tell her. She'd be kind. It would never be just about money. She circled the Appaloosa slowly, ran her fingers through his brown mane, and when he lifted his head, planted a kiss on the flat of his velvety nose. She drew a deep breath and spoke up. "He's really mine?"

Eyes bright, her parents looked at one another, then Mom dipped her head into the crook of Dad's shoulder. A light breeze carried the sweet smell of apples.

"Looks to me," Griff said, "like he always was."